BLOOD FLAME

Blood Flame: The Flame Series - Book 1

By Caris Roane

Formatting and cover by Bella Media Management.

ISBN-13: 978-1519113160

BLOOD FLAME

The Blood Flame Series - Book 1

Caris Roane

Dear Reader,

Welcome to the first installment of the Flame Series, BLOOD FLAME!

Connor, a powerful vampire serving as a Border Patrol Officer for his corrupt world, falls for a gifted witch who has the ability to kill him with a single touch...

In this book, vampire Officer Connor of the Crescent Border Patrol tries to suppress his desire for the powerful witch, Iris Meldeere. Because the woman possesses the ability to kill him with the tips of her fingers, how can he possibly fall in love with her? When a double homicide throws them together, he soon finds his deepest fantasies fulfilled as Iris succumbs to his seductions. But as they battle together to stay alive, and love begins to consume them both, will the witch be able to forgive the dark secrets of his past ...

Enjoy!

Caris Roane

For the *latest releases* and *coolest contests,* be sure to sign up for my newsletter!!!

http://www.carisroane.com/contact-2/

Now Available: AMETHYST FLAME, the second book in The Flame Series

http://www.carisroane.com/amethyst-flame-2/

Now Available: EMBRACE THE HUNT, Book 8 of the Blood Rose Series

A powerful vampire warrior. A beautiful fae of great ability. A war that threatens to destroy their love for the second time...

http://www.carisroane.com/8-embrace-the-hunt/

Coming Soon: EMBRACE THE POWER, the final installment of the Blood Rose Series!

Be sure to check out the Blood Rose Tales Box Set – TRAPPED, HUNGER, and SEDUCED -- shorter works for a quick, sexy, satisfying read. For more information: http://www.carisroane.com/blood-rose-tales-box-set/

CHAPTER ONE

Connor held a spotting scope pressed to his eye. His adrenaline flowed as he levitated high in the air. He was forty feet above the witch, his heart pounding in his chest. He'd tried about a dozen times to leave, but couldn't since his craving for the Tribunal Public Safety officer had finally tipped the needle into the red zone. He wanted her bad.

As a Border Patrol officer for Crescent Territory, he often spent time surveilling suspects. The problem was Iris Meldeere hadn't broken the law. She wasn't part of a Five Bridges drug cartel, she didn't traffic innocent humans into their sick world, and she definitely kept her hands off the lucrative business of running flame drugs.

For a witch, she was a model citizen.

It was after midnight, but he was still in the middle of his shift. And he had no damn reason to be at Iris's house, except he couldn't help himself. Not that he had plans for the future since he could never actually be with the woman. As a witch, and a powerful one at that, she had the power to kill him with a touch of her fingers.

She moved around her overgrown garden, her voice reaching his ears almost incessantly. At first, he thought she was talking to someone on her Bluetooth because both hands were constantly busy, pruning, digging, cutting, planting. He'd rolled his eyes when he realized she was communicating with her plants. Very witch or very Iris, maybe both.

Apart from his bizarre need to spy on the woman, he hated witches with a passion.

A witch had started this whole shitfest with a brew pot. Result?

1

Seventy thousand humans, in Phoenix alone, lived in a pit of hell, having gone through the *alter* and become something not human anymore. At least the original witch had changed as well. Witches were now one of the five *alter* species living in Five Bridges. Being an *alter* witch or a vampire wasn't a choice; it was a genetic mutation.

His own story wasn't unusual. Devastated by his wife's death, he'd stupidly tried to numb-out with a hit of blood flame. But it had been laced with the *alter* serum that created a set of fangs and an annoying craving for blood. The flame drugs by themselves weren't the culprit, only when enhanced with an *alter* serum.

He'd gained physical strength and long-life. Beyond that, he was living a nightmare, one that had started thirty years ago, not long after the flame drug craze had hit the human population.

Now he was here, watching a witch who had gotten hit with an *alter* serum herself ten years ago. Only her flame drug had carried the witch serum. He knew this because he'd Googled her. A lot.

She wore a purple smock over her jeans and a pair of flats that looked like ballet shoes, typical brew-faring clothes for one of her kind.

And he liked her in jeans. She wore them snug and that was part of the problem. He'd seen her dozens of times at the Tribunal building in her casual investigative uniform of short-sleeved t-shirt, also worn tight, along with the form-fitting jeans. He'd mentally stripped her clothes off about a thousand times. He swore he knew what she looked like naked.

Yeah. Obsessed.

And guilty as hell. His kind didn't go with her kind.

His kind *killed* witches, wizards and anything else that dared to smash up herbs and throw them in a cauldron, or cast spells, or worse, kill with the tips of their fingers. Witches, like Iris, were a danger to vampires and shifters. She should be offed, like all her murdering, enthralling kind.

Yet, here he was, floating above her garden, so quiet he'd never be heard not even by another vampire. He'd gotten good at stalking the woman.

Iris had that feeling again across the top of her shoulders that a vampire was watching her. She had excellent instincts, but every time she either hunted through her garden or checked the night sky, nothing.

She also had an instinct about who the vampire was. James Connor, also known as Officer Connor, of the Crescent Territory Border Patrol.

Yep, Connor was here again, which caused her heart to beat hard in her chest. Vampires killed witches as often as they could, but in this case an attack wasn't what she feared.

No, the dull thuds of her pulse meant something far worse. Against all reason, small tendrils of pure desire moved over her breasts, down the insides of her thighs and curled around her sex.

A year ago, she'd seen Connor at a crime scene, one that involved a couple of human children. Until that moment, she would never have believed a vampire capable of any kind of compassion. She honestly thought that the *alter* had removed all tender emotions from those humans who had become vampire.

That night, she'd been called to the same scene to make a full report on behalf of the Five Bridges Tribunal, the central governing organization for which she worked. She served as a Tribunal Public Safety officer and as such could move freely among all five territories without too much fear of getting assassinated in the process. Murder among the five *alter* species was rampant.

At the crime scene, with so many vampires present, she'd remained in the shadows, content to merely observe and gather data.

Because of the bloodsuckers, her own killing instinct had risen to the surface, vibrating like a motorcycle engine on overdrive. Her fingers had ached to touch some pressure-points that night and rid her world of a few sets of fangs.

She hated this aspect of being a witch, the driving need to strike another species down. But every one of her kind, once having gone through the *alter*, felt an intense pressure to self-protect. She'd come to accept that what she experienced was a basic survival mechanism. Vampires and shifters killed witches, her kind returned the favor, though for her she'd only done so when attacked. However, that didn't change how much she detested her new nature.

The crime scene that night had torn her own heart into a thousand pieces. Two children were found at the Phoenix entrance to Sentinel Bridge, a boy and a girl, about nine or ten. They'd accidentally gotten hold of one of the flame drugs that carried the *alter* serum, and had begun the process of change. But children couldn't handle the sudden physical trauma involved. Death always followed.

They'd held hands as they'd died, facing each other. It had broken Iris's heart, seeing their twisted bodies, fingers entwined. She'd wept quietly, and that's when Connor had arrived.

She'd seen him many times at various crime scenes, but never like this. He'd taken one look at the pair then dropped to his knees, covered his chest with both arms and rocked. She'd had no idea what had gone through his head at that moment, but she'd felt his compassion in waves hitting her over and over, wrecking her heart and somehow causing her to become fixated on a damn vampire.

As much as she'd come to loathe his kind, she'd ended up craving him with a terrible need.

She was tired of thinking about him almost constantly, though. More often than not, her thoughts turned into elaborate fantasies that usually involved his fangs buried in her neck and his cock plunging in and out of her sex. Sick as hell.

Tonight, she was determined to change all that.

With a fresh lime in her hands, she moved into her workroom between the house and her garden. She set about creating a spell that she should have used about eleven months and four weeks ago. She had no doubt, once completed, the formula would end her obsession.

She fired up her cast iron pot-belly stove, using elder wood. Once blazing, she placed the blade portion of her hatchet on top. She needed the metal hot enough to slice instantly through a thick wax candle.

On her worktable, she cut the lime in half, then squeezed the juice onto a purified elder wood tray. She rolled a thick black candle in the juice and invoked Connor's name several times until she felt the spell move into place. At the same time, she made use of one of her most powerful incantations. She then picked up the heated hatchet and held it aloft ready to slam the blade through the thick wax and break Connor's hold on her.

She felt her witch power racing through her veins, giving her a heady buzz. The swirl of electrified energy let her know how potent the spell was. She had no doubt it would work.

With her arm poised and ready to strike, a soft longing ran through her of things hidden behind the veil of death. Her sister came to mind and she felt, as she often did, a trail of loving fingers down both cheeks.

She closed her eyes, her throat tight. "Violet. Are you here?"

A wind from the garden whipped through the room, smelling of thyme, the herb of love she always associated with her sister. Tears tracked down her cheeks.

Violet was long dead, killed in a vampire massacre nine years ago. Yet, in this moment her sister's spirit was here, in Iris's workroom.

"Violet," she whispered again.

Once more, the wind blew in a strong gust and the scent of thyme thickened in the air. "Don't you want me to end this obsession?"

This time, the fingers once more touched her cheeks while the wind blew. *No-o-o-o,* came softly into her mind.

Iris talked with Violet a lot, but her sister had never communicated with words before, not once in all these years. Yet, she had now.

"Violet?" She looked around, wondering if the ghost would show herself.

But nothing happened, no fingers on her face, no words in her mind, nothing.

She lowered the hatchet and returned it to a slab of cast iron on the long butcher block counter near the sink. It would need time and a safe place to cool.

She felt frightened suddenly. Something was coming and Violet was part of it, as was Connor. She walked back out to her garden to try to calm down, but again she sensed Connor was near, watching her.

But why? She knew the reasons she'd fallen into an obsession with him, but why did he so often hover above her house?

~ ~ ~

Connor's com vibrated against his shoulder. For the moment, he ignored it because Iris had finally returned to the garden. His whole vampire being was focused on her. He wanted her sex and he wanted her blood. And in a strange way, he longed to talk with her.

He stared down at her as she lifted her gaze once more in his direction, hunting through the night sky. But he knew she wouldn't be able to see him. All vampires had the means to remain partially cloaked from witches, one of the few defenses they had against Iris's kind. The distance completed his invisibility.

Using his scope, he centered it on her face once more. Damn, she was beautiful and that was part of the problem. He'd always preferred dark-haired women and her large, brown eyes had a soulful expression he knew reflected her nature, despite that she was a witch.

He knew a lot about her because he'd hunted her down on the Internet and made an illegal search of her home computer. He knew which websites she visited, that she followed a blog called, 'Witches and Self-Awareness', and her Tumblr page had lots of pictures of animals, the forest, and travel photos of Europe.

He even knew the porn site she preferred, which had been fodder for his fantasies over the past two months. Iris, of course, played the lead.

He really was just this side of stalking.

Hell, who was he kidding? He was stalking Iris, though to be fair he had no intention of ever intruding into her life.

An owl swooped down on her suddenly, then took up his usual perch in the huge tree at the back of her yard.

Her melodious voice hit the air once more. "Hello, Sebastien." He could hear Iris laughing and talking with the owl, her pet, or muse or whatever it was witches used to conjure shit.

When his com buzzed for the second time, he swiftly rose another thirty feet in the air then pressed the button. "Connor."

"Talking pretty quiet. You on a stake-out?"

He recognized Lily's voice and some of the tension eased out of him. Lily worked dispatch, manning the phones and passing out assignments. "Trying not to attract notice."

"So, who is she?"

The question startled him. He didn't think anybody knew what he did between calls. Shit.

Then he realized Lily was fishing. "A beautiful Honda Scrambler, 1973." Half true. He'd started to collect Café Racers, the older, the better.

He heard Lily snort. "You men and your machines. Okay, listen up. This comes from the chief. We've got a runner out at Amado Bridge and he wants you on it."

Connor frowned. He didn't usually work the dead-talker end of vampire territory. "Isn't that Jason's section?"

"Jason's MIA, has been for two nights now, and the chief is about ready to explode."

Unusual for Jason to be missing, but he was a Border Patrol officer and sometimes the men needed to go on a bender just to survive. "He'll turn up, but his head won't feel too good."

Lily laughed. "I totally agree and to answer your next question, yes, Easton was adamant you take this call."

No point arguing about any decision the chief made. "I'm on it."

He took off, heading north in the direction of Crescent Territory, wondering what the hell he would find this time. He touched the hilt of his half-sword and thumbed the holster of his Glock. He wore black leather wrist guards lined with steel, a black tank, leathers, and heavy boots. He was ready.

Amado Bridge. He scowled. One of the worst terrains for a runner to attempt to take drugs into the human world.

His instincts lit up. Jason was missing, a runner was out at Amado and Easton wanted him on the assignment.

A sick feeling started crawling around his gut. This call already stunk and it was only midnight. Great.

~~ * ~~

At the same moment Iris felt Connor take off, her cell rang. She fished it from her jeans pocket and saw that the Tribunal was calling. She frowned because she wasn't working tonight, and she had a dozen orders to fill. Her job as a TPS officer barely paid the bills so she supplemented her income by creating special potions. Using a human dealer, she had her products selling at high prices in the various malls and specialty stores around Phoenix. She was doing well.

She touched the phone face. "Meldeere."

"Sorry, Sweetie, but Donaldson wants you out at Amado Bridge." Faith doled out the assignments through the night and had a calming effect with the officers. "Know where that is?"

"Northwest Crescent Territory."

"Right."

Iris frowned. "But I'm not on duty."

"I told his royal highness as much, but his face turned red, you know in that fucked up wizard way of his. He then let a few choice words fly. I tossed up both my hands and said I'd give you a shout."

Donaldson was a prick, no question about that. He was also corrupt as hell, so already Iris was uneasy. Corruption tended to lead to the three drug-lords in Five Bridges. But her fingers were squeaky clean so she couldn't imagine why any of them would send her out there. "What's the crime?"

"Some Border Patrol officer has gone berserk. Donaldson wants it documented and you have permission to take the BP's ass out if you find him abusing the perp, which would be awesome."

Crescent Territory was home to the *alter* vampires, which meant all Crescent Border Patrol officers were vampires.

Iris chuckled. She liked Faith. "You're not being very politically correct. We're supposed to honor all five species. Didn't you get the memo?"

"What-the-fuck-evuh. Do us proud. Got another call."

Iris put her phone back and started stripping off her smock. With her Sig Sauer clipped to her belt, she headed to her garage and revved up her TPS motorcycle. It was a big, heavy Harley-Davidson police cruiser, a bike fit for carting her around all five territories, including No Man's Land. She wished she could fly like some of the more powerful vampire officers and a couple of the witches who served in Elegance's Border Patrol. She didn't have the gift of levitation, at least not yet. Maybe one day, if she lived long enough.

But she liked the bike, even though it was more machine than she needed. Although, it worked well for the bigger male bodies on the TPS force.

As she headed out, taking her quiet street at a low rumble, she wondered why she'd been called to Amado Bridge when there were at least a dozen witches and wizards on duty right now at the Trib station.

~~ * ~~

Connor had a flame-runner in his sights, an emaciated female with the telltale marks of drug-use blazing on her neck. He could see the tattoo-like flames. Hers were dark red, so he knew which cocktail she'd been using to get her head swimming: blood flame.

Because she was drug-running, he had every right as a Border Patrol officer to put a bullet in the back of her head. All three drug-lords preferred it as well. Prevented snitching.

But he never pulled the trigger unless he knew exactly what he was dealing with. He'd learned his lesson the hard way. Guilt still clawed at him, ripping him apart on a nightly basis, even though the incident was over nine-years-old now. He shuddered as the memory tried to push to the front of his head, but he shoved it back.

He levitated with long practice, his head bent slightly, arm raised as he gazed down his sights. Jesus, the woman was clawing her way up the steep side of the wash, weighed down by a loaded runner jacket. She must not have known the area.

So what was she doing out here? Runners by occupation were sneaky bastards, using tunnels that often collapsed on them to get from the cordoned off area of Five Bridges to Phoenix. The flame drugs, as well as the *alter* serums that could be added to the drugs, had transformed a fifteen square mile section of North Phoenix into five territories, each partitioned from the next with barbed wire then separated from Phoenix in the same way. The National Guard patrolled the external border of the entire circumference of Five Bridges.

He worked the internal border of Crescent Territory, trying to keep any of the numerous flame drugs from leaving Five Bridges.

That same sick feeling crawled through his stomach again.

He touched his shoulder com. "I've got eyes on the runner at Amado Bridge, but she's a pretty weak female. Shall I bring her in?" Maybe Easton would want a say in this tonight.

When he got no answer on his shoulder com, he tried again.

And again.

He'd been disconnected.

Yeah. Something was off.

The runner was the key. And like hell he was going to serve as some asshole's assassin, even if it was Easton himself who wanted the woman dead.

He holstered his gun and cursed. He needed to have a talk with her.

Levitating swiftly, he shot through the air. Gauging the distance, he caught her jacket at the back of the neck and lifted her up. She screamed as he carried her flailing to the upper edge of the wash and flung her into the dirt.

"What are you doing out here, runner?"

The woman didn't move. She lay face down, one hand digging into the weeds. Her head was inches away from a stand of prickly pear.

She mumbled something, but he couldn't hear her.

"Say again? You sound like you have rocks in your mouth."

She lifted her head up. "Just kill us. We'll both be better off."

"Us?" He drew his gun again, holding it in both hands. He bent his knees and pivoted in a 360. Nothing. Except a witch on the bridge watching him. He stopped the moment he saw the woman. Why was she there?

Then he recognized the familiar dark ponytail. Holy fuck, it was Iris, but what was she doing on Amado Bridge?

He turned his attention back to the runner. "I don't see anyone else. Who's 'us', Ma'am? You got someone out here running with you?"

"Yes, but you're looking in the wrong place."

She wasn't making sense. Blood flame had no doubt screwed with her mind.

"I'll ask again; where's your friend?"

"Here."

Glancing down, he watched her turn on her side. She held her arm at the bottom of the coat, pressing it against her body.

When he saw the bulge of her stomach, his mind flipped over several times. The memory he'd been trying to suppress shot forward once more of another woman running flame.

Connor had killed her, shot her in the chest as she turned, gun in hand and pointed straight at him. He hadn't hesitated.

But the gun had been taped to her wrist and she couldn't have fired it if she'd wanted to. A set-up.

She'd also been pregnant, just like this one.

Darkness swirled through his head, a familiar creeping of more regrets than any man should have to bear. He'd killed her and others equally as innocent over the years until his soul was as dark as night. The flame drugs had been at the bottom of it all. He'd gone through the change and become something he despised.

"You gonna shoot, or what?"

Coming back to himself, he shook his head then holstered his Glock.

Five Bridges had worn him down to the marrow. But right now he knew something sinister was going on, directed at him and involving a drug addict lying in the dirt.

He shifted toward Iris. Was she involved in some way? Had she set him up? As a TPS officer, she had access to a lot of important people. The Tribunal was the combined government for all five species and held sway over each of the five separate territories as well as their individual border patrols.

It wasn't a question he could answer right now, so he shifted back to the runner and extended a hand down to her. She eyed it as though it would turn into a snake any second.

"Come on. I haven't got all night. Let's get you out of here. You're not dying on my watch."

He didn't kill women, at least not on purpose, and he definitely didn't take out a woman with a belly full of child.

"I can't move." She tried to sit up, but flopped back in the dirt.

Whatever energy she'd possessed had been used up trying to scale the fairly steep side of the wash.

He dipped down and picked her up in his arms, cradling her. She weighed next to nothing. "What's your name?"

"Tammy. Where are you taking me?"

"The clinic."

She turned her face against his chest and damn him if she didn't start weeping against his tank.

But as he rose into the air, he glanced once more at Iris. She had her pistol pointed at him, head bent slightly, probably checking her sights.

Though the clinic was the opposite direction, he flew toward her. She slowly lowered her gun.

By the time he reached the bridge, her eyes were wide, her lips parted. "Officer Connor."

"Officer Meldeere. What the fuck are you doing out here?" He might be obsessed with her and he'd definitely engaged in way too many fantasies about her, but she was still a witch with a gun.

"Got a call that some Border Patrol officer was out of control near Amado Bridge."

"Do I look out of control?"

Her gaze fell to the woman. "No. You don't."

"Guess you won't be shooting me, then."

She shook her head. She looked amazing, a flush on her cheeks. Her eyes glittered as she stared at him.

If he didn't know better …

Fuck this. He whipped around and flew swiftly toward the clinic. He had to find some damn way of getting Iris out of his head.

He just didn't know how.

He also needed to find out who had sent Tammy drug-running in the western sector of his territory.

~~ * ~~

Iris holstered her Sig. Her arms and legs trembled but it wasn't from fear. Damn Connor. He'd just proven himself all over again, helping a woman like that.

And she'd forgotten how blue his eyes were.

She could hardly breathe and all she'd done was look at him and exchange about a half-dozen words. He wore the usual black tank, so his tattoos stood out like beacons. He was heavily muscled like all the Border Patrol men. How many times had she wondered if both hands together would fit around one of his biceps?

Fortunately, now that he was no longer next to her, she could think again. She looked around. On Trib orders, she'd left her garden, her owl and the potions she needed to make to fill her orders, but for what? She didn't get it. Why had Donaldson wanted her witnessing Connor's supposed crime?

The situation was just weird enough to force her to ask the harder questions: Who had really sent her out to Amado Bridge? And if the purpose had been to kill Connor, then why? And why her?

She turned the key in her bike and revved up her Harley once more. She took off, loving the strong vibrations on her bottom as she swept onto the street, heading toward Del Muerto Bridge. Del Muerto was one of the five main bridges of her world and connected Crescent with the dead-talker province of Shadow Territory.

With her long hair in a ponytail, she enjoyed the feel of the night wind as she moved along. She only had to head over to the Tribunal building and fill out a report, then she could return to her workroom.

In the meantime, she loved riding.

When she was well into the land of dead-talkers, whipping through some backstreets and racing over several smaller bridges, her com buzzed. She pressed her shoulder transmitter. "Meldeere."

She heard Faith's voice. "We've got a ... out on Sentinel Bridge. The ... Donal ... wants you ... now."

She repressed a sigh. The Tribunal meant well, but dammit, couldn't they invest in a decent com system? "Say again?"

After three more repeated requests, she finally got the gist. There was some kind of incident on Sentinel Bridge which connected Connor's Territory and hers.

And once more, the chief wanted her out there. She almost asked Faith why, but figured she'd get the same response.

"On my way."

"Say ..." More static then a lot of broken up words.

Iris shut off her com with a heavy eye-roll and put on some speed.

"Well, Violet, what do you think?" She tended to talk to her sister when she was out on patrol.

But the spontaneous question, took her straight back to the wind that had blown through her workroom and hearing Violet's voice in her head. Tears burned her eyes. Violet had been buried a long time ago, but for Iris, the memory was as sharp as yesterday.

Thinking about her sister, however, brought the past surging forward. Several months after their shared *alter*, Violet had gone to work at a sandwich shop in downtown Elegance. Without warning, she and a dozen other witches had been abducted by a number of drugged out vampires. They'd been hauled out to a place called No Man's Land, also known as the Graveyard.

The vampires had been out of control and hyped up on blood flame. The witches' hands had been bound to prevent the witch death touch. The women had been stabbed, choked, raped and drained to death.

The Tribunal investigation had gone on for years but died its own death some time later. It had been buried in the Trib's paperwork morgue, no doubt at the request of one of the drug-lords.

No closure for nine years, just pain.

She traversed yet another small bridge, the bike thump-thumping at the entrance and exit.

The world of Five Bridges had about a hundred bridges scattered throughout the ripped up territory of north-central Phoenix, most of them short and only one lane wide. Long ditches crisscrossed the land, a final containment solution to the ongoing drug and human trafficking problem that had accompanied the flame revolution. The hundreds of ditches were as difficult to traverse as they were completely ineffective in stemming the export of flame drugs to the human world.

Many of the original homes in this part of Phoenix now served the citizens of Five Bridges. But at least half had been blasted away and the pits left to grow whatever the desert could manage. Or they'd been dozed out even more to create rows of ditches hard to navigate on foot. A lot of cactus took root in these places. Rattlesnakes and vermin set up camp in droves. Coyotes, too. More bridges were built, some as short as seven feet.

Five Bridges essentially had the look of a war zone, especially with barbed wire separating each of the five territories from each other as well as from Phoenix. There were a few beauty spots in some of the renovated areas or in backyards like her own. Otherwise, it was a place that looked like bombs were detonated on a regular basis and the rubble left to sprout any weed or grass that would survive without much water.

There were, however, five main bridges, hence the name for the cesspool she lived in. Sentinel was one of them, the bridge she was headed to now. It was the long, main bridge connecting Crescent with her witch world of Elegance. It also intersected with the human world as all five bridges did, in a T layout. It still amazed Iris that any human would want to come to Five Bridges. But then most who did were looking for drugs or sex, the latter the second most important source of revenue for the poorer residents.

Now there was an unspecified incident on Sentinel Bridge.

So much for being off duty.

~~ * ~~

At the clinic, Connor leaned over Tammy, who proved to be an un-*altered* human female, working the sex trade in Five Bridges. He was trying to catch her words. She mumbled a lot and slipped in and out of consciousness since she was still tangled up with blood flame.

"What were you doing out there, Tammy? I could tell you had no idea where you were going."

"He told me to go out there or he'd kill me."

"Who?"

"The man who gave me the drugs. I owed him."

The baby was hooked up to a fetal heart monitor and its heart beat fast and steady. The nurse stood nearby and scowled. Working in a clinic like this, she'd no doubt seen it all. The baby, if it survived, would have to go through withdrawal.

"Tammy, focus. What did the man look like?"

She lifted a weak hand to her right shoulder. "Skull tattoo, here, the kind with the mouth wide open like it's screaming."

"Bald head with tats?"

"Yes. And a really big nose. And super tight pants."

Connor held back a curse. He knew the small-time player. His name was Gary Smith and he owned the House of Big Sex in Rotten Row. Connor and his crew called him Big Nuts because he wore tight pants to display an oversized scrotum, an unfortunate look on any man.

But why had the owner of a sex club sent a woman out in a fake runner jacket? What game was he playing at?

"You need to leave." The nurse's voice blasted through the room like it came out of a sawed off shotgun. "We're going to put her under. There's too much stress on her heart because of the drug. The baby's at risk."

Connor dipped his chin in response. He had what he needed anyway, the name of the man who'd set him up. He picked up the runner jacket loaded with nothing but fake bricks and vials, another indication someone was messing with him.

When he reached the admitting desk, he talked to a lovely vampire he knew well, a woman he'd slept with a few months ago. She'd already touched his hand a couple of times and had a look in her eye he knew well. His gaze slipped to her throat where she was not-so-subtly stroking her fingers over her vein.

Because of his constant lust for Iris, his groin lit up with sudden need. He almost asked where they could go to have a private chat.

But his com buzzed, the connection finally restored. He hit the button. "Connor."

Lily's voice came on. "How did things go out at Amado?"

He explained about the young woman and that he'd brought her to the clinic.

Lily was silent for a moment. "You know, you stand taller than every other man I know." She cleared her voice and hurried on. "But I guess this is your lucky night. We've got an incident out at Sentinel Bridge. A homicide, and yes, Chief wants you out there, as well. Pronto."

He never worked Sentinel either.

What the fuck was going on?

~~ * ~~

Iris stood over not one, but two bodies on Sentinel Bridge, a man and a woman. Over the years, she'd seen a lot of corpses, but nothing quite as bad as the cuts, bruises, and burns on this pair. She forced herself to swallow and keep swallowing.

Despite the extensive damage, she recognized the female. She knew her, though not well, a witch by the name of Sadie Thompson. Her throat had been cut, and except for the severe bruising, her skin was the color of white marble.

The man was a vampire, something she knew by instinct though on the surface he looked like any other man, no matter the species. The *alter* had given her discernment as it did all Five Bridges citizens. She always knew what was what.

She had no idea who he was, though. His dark hair was fanned over the side of his face. He wore the leather pants the Border Patrol men wore, so there was a good chance he served on the Crescent force. He had burns all down his arms and chest, along with severe bruising, and enough cuts to finally bleed him out.

Her stomach knotted up. She had to look away, regroup.

She focused on the tri-part bridge itself and each of three sets of entrance-exist gates. A 'T' formation occurred in the center of the bridge and led to east Phoenix. This part was guarded by the US Border Patrol. The main bridge itself served to connect Elegance Territory with Crescent.

Witches and wizards lived in Elegance exclusively. Vampires in Crescent.

Right now, Sentinel Bridge looked like something out of a movie, with a dozen cop cars lit up, lights flashing at all three control points. The closest vehicle was maybe forty yards away.

But why had Donaldson wanted her out here? What possible good could come from her presence? She was only sent to witness a case like this, make a report, and offer suggestions about follow-up, most of which would never be acted on. One of the Border Patrol stations would handle the case itself. She had no significant role, except possibly in identifying the Elegance victim.

She stood alone in the center of the bridge, her bike a few yards away. She'd already spoken with the Elegance Border Patrol officers who'd been directed to wait for her, but at a serious distance. According to them, the vampires were sending a man in to have a look.

She put a hand to her chest and walked in a slow circle. In the distance, she caught sight of a Crescent officer levitating above the flashing police cars. He was heading in the direction of the crime scene.

Now she'd have to deal with a macho vampire, who'd no doubt give her grief because she was a witch.

Returning to the two victims, she set her gaze on the dead vampire. He was bare-chested and like most BP officers, had lots of tattoos. He was lean and heavily muscled. His pants were cut up badly in a number of places.

She had so many questions. Why were the two of them placed here? Were they involved in some way? And how the hell could any of the drug lords orchestrate this kind of closing of Sentinel in order to put the couple in position? The Tribunal had charge of the five major bridges.

From her peripheral, she saw the vampire land. She turned toward him and lost the ability to breathe all over again. "Connor."

Holy shit, the second time tonight. The third if she counted his hovering above her house. But why was he out here now?

"Iris." He'd never looked more startled as he stared at her. "You were called to Sentinel? *You* specifically?"

"I was. And you?"

He nodded.

Her mind spun. "Is Sentinel part of the territory you usually cover?"

"Nope." He was scowling hard.

"I wasn't even supposed to be on duty tonight."

He shook his head. "Why are either of us here? This makes no sense."

"I totally agree with you."

His gaze fell to the couple. "They've been tortured."

She nodded in agreement, but had to work at swallowing again.

When he shifted his gaze back to her, she found it hard to breathe. She didn't know what he was thinking, but like hell she was going to look away first.

She knew the game. Vampires valued strength above just about everything else and one thing the battling of his kind had made her: *She was damn strong.*

His jaw worked and his eyes narrowed as he finally shifted his gaze once more to the couple on the pavement. "So what do we have here?"

Iris looked at the wrecked bodies once more. "I have no idea."

He waved a hand toward the woman. "And she's a witch."

"Yes. Sadie Thompson. She worked at the Tribunal, though in a different department." She took a deep breath. "I didn't know her well, but I understand she was a good, hard working woman."

He glanced at Iris, his lips twisted in disgust.

Right. Vampires hated her kind as much as she despised his. In his view, there was no such thing as a *good witch*, so what did he mean by hovering above her house as often as he did? Was he spying on her?

He walked slowly toward the bodies, scowling. Leaning down, he pulled the hair back from the vampire's face then let loose with a long string of obscenities.

Connor knew him.

"He's a Border Patrol officer, isn't he?"

"Yes. Jason. He's only been missing a couple of days. I thought he just needed to let off some steam. Christ, who would do this to a BP man?" For the most part, even the drug-lords let the officers alone, except to bribe those they could, of course.

She frowned at Connor. Was he on the take? Somehow, she doubted it. A man who would carry a runner to a clinic wouldn't take bribes.

The earliest questions resurfaced in her mind. Why had both she and Connor been called to Sentinel Bridge?

CHAPTER TWO

Connor stared down at Jason, his chest tight. All Border Patrol officers made enemies, usually a member of one of the Five Bridges cartels.

But it was rare for an officer to be killed outright. Connor knew of instances where officers simply disappeared never to be seen again. One thing the drug bosses excelled at was keeping a low profile.

Which made this incident a quandary. There was nothing subtle about two dead bodies on Sentinel Bridge.

He squatted on his haunches to get a closer look. There would be no forensics team. His world didn't bother with serious investigations. And as far as the human world was concerned, every citizen of Five Bridges could go four-hooves-up and no one would give a damn.

But Connor needed at least a few questions answered. "Iris, I'm going to have a look at Jason. Just a warning. You might want to turn your back."

"Thanks, but I'm good."

He glanced up at her. The woman had strength. Another thing he liked about the witch, damn it.

Reverting his attention back to his fallen comrade, he slid his hands under Jason's back then tilted him onto his side. He held him in that position, not wanting him to fall forward.

What he saw made his stomach churn. Jason had been hung up on meat-hooks then beaten with something more than a pair of fists. Metal pipes, maybe. Other deep cuts went past his waistband. He didn't want to think about where they led.

He carefully laid Jason back down. He couldn't hurt him now; he was long dead. But he felt a profound need to be gentle. He took a couple of deep breaths, an ache in his throat.

He examined Jason's hands for other signs of torture. His nails were intact though several of his fingers were broken. He also had a red, half-heart tattoo between his forefinger and thumb.

Curious, Connor glanced at the witch's hand.

And there it was.

He stood up. Was it possible? "Holy shit," he murmured.

"What?" Iris moved in closer.

Connor waved his hand between the bodies. "These two were involved."

"Why on earth would you say that? Wait a minute, what did you see?"

"They have a shared tattoo, two red half-hearts. If you put them together, you get a whole."

Iris shifted to have a look herself, then returned to stand once more beside Connor. She shook her head as though unable to make sense of what she'd seen. "But that would mean—"

Apparently, she couldn't even speak the words. Truth was, he had a hard time saying it as well. "They were lovers."

She shook her head again, harder this time. "No, that's not possible. He's a vampire."

He totally got where she was coming from. "And she's a witch." He met her gaze and a strong current passed between them.

He felt as though a pulse of energy kept hitting his sternum repeatedly. She must have experienced something similar because she drew in a soft stream of air and immediately folded her arms across her chest as though protecting herself.

"Are you trying to enthrall me?"

Her eyes popped wide. "No. God, no. I would never do something like that."

"But you could."

"Yes, but I wouldn't."

He believed her, which meant he was in serious trouble. He trusted the witch and his instincts told him this bizarre thing between them was mutual.

"You knew I was at your house tonight, didn't you?"

She huffed a sigh. "I did."

"Were you always aware? Each time I came to you?" He'd gone past counting the number of times he'd hovered above her garden, making liberal use of his spotting scope.

She nodded slowly, frowning. "Yet, you never approached me or tried to hurt me. The visits seemed harmless enough." Her eyes glittered. "Fuck."

"What's going on, Connor? I don't get any of this, as in why you've been spying on me or this strange attraction between us. I mean, did you arrange to have me brought here to Sentinel?"

"I don't have those kinds of connections or power."

"Well, why did you start coming to my house in the first place? I don't get it?"

He turned toward her and took her arm in a firm grip. He felt a flow of energy race up and down his arm, something he couldn't explain. "Because of this. Do you feel it?"

She nodded. "It's some kind of visceral reaction. So you're saying you were at my house because you're attracted to me, even though I'm a witch."

"*Despite* that you're a witch."

She stared at him for a long moment. She was so beautiful with her large brown eyes and high cheekbones. For a weird moment, he saw down the years and she was with him, really with him.

Which seemed impossible. He couldn't be with any woman, not after what he'd done in No Man's Land.

When he released her, she didn't move away from him, but kept looking at him.

"What?"

"I don't know what this is between us, but it feels very old as though it's always existed."

Her words reminded him that she was a witch, one more reason a relationship with her could never work. He shifted his gaze back to Jason.

"Connor." Her voice was low, compassionate.

"Forget it. I shouldn't have pushed things." He gestured to the bodies. "What we need to figure out is how you and I are connected to this murder."

"I think you're right."

Connor thought about Jason. He'd known him for at least fifteen years. He then considered Tammy for a moment and the similarity to Connor's killing of the pregnant woman.

"Shit."

"What?"

"I don't know if the two things are connected, but Jason was with me on another night a long time ago. An incident involving an un-*altered* human who was pregnant like Tammy. This woman, whose name I still don't know, had been set-up. At the time, I was acting instinctively and when she turned with a gun in her hand, I shot and killed her. Jason was there. He was with me that night." He didn't add that the event had ruined something inside him.

He couldn't look at Iris. Most of the time he felt normal, or as normal as a vampire could ever feel. But when these memories intruded, darkness engulfed Connor. He'd become something he despised, a killer of the innocent. He was unworthy of any good thing this life could offer.

Staring back at him, in the form of these dead lovers, was love, something he would never know, not in this life. He wasn't deserving on any level.

Suddenly, Iris clutched his arm. "Connor!" Her voice carried panic. He turned to her. "What?"

She released his arm and spread her hands wide, but stared down at her feet or maybe at the bridge pavement. He knew witches sometimes had a sixth sense about things. "What's going on?"

She met his gaze, her dark eyes panicky. "The stones of the bridge structure are talking to me. I know you don't trust me because I'm a witch, but can you levitate us the hell out of here? This bridge is going to blow."

He didn't think twice, but picked her up and shot into the air. He flew straight up and as he did a deafening boom shattered the night sky. The resulting force blasted him hard, propelling him higher and higher. Bridge shrapnel bruised him but good. He could feel his pants getting ripped to shreds, though his boots seemed to be holding steady.

The witch held him tight, both arms wrapped around his neck, her head buried against his shoulder. Flying pieces of pavement kept hitting him, most ricocheting off the bottom of his boots. They had to be delivering up some hurt to her as well.

"How you doin'?"

"My ass. Jesus H. Christ, that hurts!"

He had no idea who'd set the bomb, but he was pretty sure it was meant for him and for Iris, too. What he couldn't figure out was why. Who would want them both dead?

~~ * ~~

Iris trembled for more than one reason. She hurt, the bomb had scared her to death, and she had her arms wrapped around Connor. And he was the source of way too many fantasies that could never be fulfilled.

"Can you loosen your grip?" he asked, his voice sounding hoarse.

"Yes." She slowly released the stranglehold.

The truth was, she'd never flown before and the sight of the earth so far below freaked her out.

His voice rumbled against her ear. "I've got you."

For some reason, those exact words and in the man's low timbre did something to her, made her wish her life was different.

Made her wish he was anything but a vampire.

She couldn't remember the last time she'd been this close to a man, any man. Her life in Elegance Territory and as a TPS officer had left her hardened, displaced, and alone.

"I take it you haven't been in the air before."

"No." The word came out on a squeak.

"Don't look down. It'll be easier that way."

This had all been too much. She was flying for the first time and a Trib assignment had resulted in an explosion on Sentinel Bridge. But equally unsettling was the discovery that a witch she knew had taken a vampire for a lover.

All this, in less than an hour.

She was also cut up and had to spend a lot of her energy healing the wounds on her backside and legs.

As Connor continued to fly her north, she kept her gaze fixed on the distant line of lights, where Phoenix still thrived safely beyond a heavily patrolled border. It was only a couple of miles away, but might as well have been separated by an ocean.

"Where are you taking me?" She knew they were well inside Crescent Territory. She could also feel he'd begun his descent.

"My place. I've got a few cuts and bruises I need to get fixed up and my pants are shredded. How about you?"

"My butt hurts and I'm feeling the cold air where I shouldn't."

She felt him chuckle as he descended in front of a townhouse, landing on the front porch.

Once on solid ground, she found she had a hard time letting go. The muscles in her arms were stiff from holding on. She dragged them off his shoulders and shook them out.

She'd almost died back there.

And now she owed Connor. She stared at him, trying to form a sentence to offer her gratitude, but all she did was purse her lips. Nothing would come out.

Connor frowned at her. "You're in shock. Let's get you taken care of. I have a nice Cabernet Sauvignon, if you like wine."

"Thanks." She lifted a hand, staring at it. She was shaking bad. "Jesus."

"It'll pass."

She looked up at him. "You're not upset?"

"Oh, I need some wine, too. But I've been in a lot of over-the-top situations through the years. Border Patrol isn't for sissies."

"I'm sure it isn't."

Connor slid his arm around her waist as he guided her inside his home. The kitchen was opposite the slate tiled entrance. It was very spare-looking in stainless steel, dark wood cabinets and a black granite island. The dining area was next with a small glass table and four chairs. On the far wall was a large poster of a motorcycle she recognized.

"A Ducati," she murmured. Her voice sounded dull to her own ears. Yep, shock.

"You know bikes?"

"Some. Especially the café racers. It's either been beautifully restored or is in unbelievable condition."

"I owned one before I went through the *alter*. When I had it shipped to Five Bridges, it was gone within a week. Somebody stole it, probably to use the money for flame drugs of one kind or another." He drew a deep breath. "I've acquired a couple of others since, a Honda and a Kawasaki. But one day, I hope to locate and restore a Ducati." A faraway look entered his eye. She thought she understood, especially when he added, "That is, once we have some kind of order in Crescent and the other territories."

He moved into the kitchen and pulled a bottle of wine from a tall rack housing at least twenty bottles.

"Do a lot of drinking?" She meant it as a joke, but her words came out dull and weird.

He glanced at her over his shoulder, frowning. "No. You?"

She sighed heavily. He'd just saved her life. For that alone she should cut him some slack. "I thought it would sound funny but it didn't. Sorry."

He lifted a clear glass goblet to her. "You're allowed."

As he poured, she moved close to the island and took the glass. She sipped, then moaned. "Oh, that's good."

But her throat closed up unexpectedly and she leaned over the island, a sob erupting from her throat. She set her goblet down and planted her hands over her face because she started crying for no damn good reason at all.

And she wasn't a crier.

And her ass felt thoroughly exposed and still hurt like hell.

The next thing she felt was the vampire's hand on her back, rubbing in a gentle circle. "Go ahead, let it out, Iris. You'll be the better for it."

"I don't want to cry."

"Do it anyway. My mom told me women sometimes need to let the waterworks flow to keep the lid from blowing."

She chuckled softly, because he was right.

And Connor remembered his mother, which made her really sad in another way at the same time.

So for the next few minutes, she wept. She kept feeling the rumble beneath the bridge as the old stones spoke to her, telling their horrible secret.

She should have died out there. Connor as well.

A box of tissues appeared and she blew her nose. She then rose upright, meeting his gaze. "You saved us."

"So did you." He frowned as he stared at her. "We can call it even."

"I don't think it's even at all. You didn't have to do anything. You could have just taken off and left me there, but you didn't. You picked me up."

"And you didn't have to warn me. But you did."

Her smile was crooked. "I had some self-interest in the matter."

At that, he smiled as well.

Oh, God, he was even better-looking when he showed some teeth. For a moment, she was drawn away from the disaster on the bridge. Connor was handsome as hell. His eyes were blue and intense, he had strong cheekbones, a straight nose with a sexy dip at the bridge, and arched eyebrows. He wore his dark brown hair pulled away from his face, the upper portion bound in a leather strap. The rest was wavy and hung to his shoulders. She loved the look on him.

He didn't look a day over thirty, though she knew from web-browsing that he'd been one of the early *alters* and had some years on him. Long-life had been the trade-off for the heinous change that had made him a vampire and her a witch.

She took another sip of wine then caught Connor's arm. "Thank you. Seriously. I'm more grateful than words can possibly express."

Connor couldn't breathe. The forbidden woman of his dreams had her hand on his arm and once more that strange powerful energy radiated where she touched him. He didn't want to move. He wanted to stay in this position for about a year, looking at her, feeling her hand on him.

He was nothing but grateful as well that Iris was still alive. His own ass, he hardly cared about. But Iris was a good woman, someone who should stay as far away from him as she could. If it ever made sense for her to date a vampire, he should be a last choice, not a first.

His gaze fell to her lips. He'd imagined kissing her, plunging his tongue deep, letting her feel what he really wanted to be doing.

When she sighed, he searched her eyes. She shifted toward him just enough and her breathing changed, higher in her chest.

Her lips parted.

If ever there was an invitation …

She wanted the kiss and that was something he hadn't expected. Was it possible she was into him?

"Iris?"

She blinked and caught her breath, then turned back to the island. She picked up her wine once more and took a long drink.

He'd always been certain he was alone in his interest, which in many ways had kept him safe. Now he knew something very different to be true.

His heart started pounding and he couldn't move. He should have though, because he saw the mounds of her ass through her torn clothes. He leaned close and breathed in deep. "You smell like your garden."

She chuckled, then sniffed. "And you smell like a blown up bridge with just a hint of leather." She glanced at him, her lips swollen as hell, ready to be plundered. But a sheen of tears covered her eyes once more.

What the hell was he thinking? She was feeling vulnerable and he couldn't take advantage of her. Besides, he needed to be smart. She was a witch and could kill him with one touch of her fingers to either his temple or the base of his skull.

The breath he released sounded like a hiss of steam.

He nodded, then looked away from her. His frown deepened as he rounded the island once more to pour himself a glass. He drank along with her, but stayed on the other side of the thick slab of granite. His brow had a tight, pinched feel as he stared at nothing in particular.

A change of subject would help.

He met her gaze once more. "Who would want both you and me dead? That's what I don't get. One or the other of us would make sense. I have enough enemies—"

"And your entire territory would be happy to see me in my grave."

"I won't argue with that." But his lips curved.

~~ * ~~

She wasn't offended. She knew how hard her species was on vampires, the number of massacres employed against his kind by the dark witch covens. Elegance had a number of her kind intent on destroying Crescent.

But, oh, that smile again.

He was the sort of man who pulled no punches and didn't have a lot of frills around him either. Some men needed to be hand-held. He would need something else held, but that would be about it. God help her, she liked him.

She slowly turned away from him, pretending to take in the room. She sipped her wine some more, then put her hand up against the bare parts of her ass. She flipped back around, her cheeks warming. "Have you got a long shirt or maybe a t-shirt I could borrow?"

"I do. And if you don't mind, I'm going to shower and change gear."

"Please. Do what you need to do."

Wine in hand, he moved past her, heading beyond the dining table. He was so tall, at least six-five, and built. His shoulders looked massive against his black tank. The sight of his Glock and holster clipped on one side of his belt and his half-sword with a sheath clipped to the other made her feminine soul long for more from him.

She also had a clear view of his torn up leathers and a lot of what lay beneath. Maybe he knew she was looking, but he didn't seem at all embarrassed by the rips in his pants. She wanted to look away, but couldn't and desire for him rose once more.

Her craving for him returned full force. Maybe because he wasn't standing right next to her, she felt free to indulge.

Once he disappeared down the hall, she released a heavy rush of air. Part of her was relieved to have a break from all the lust and longing. The other part was curious to discover more about him since she now had a chance to see his surroundings.

Their homes had one similarity that surprised her. Each was small, that was true. But the first room in both was the dining area.

Taking her wine with her, she moved past the table and into a small living room with black leather furniture and, not surprising, a large flatscreen TV opposite. Very male, but at the same time, he had jumbles of books stacked here and there.

She picked one up from the end table. It was a book about Egypt and the pharaohs. Beneath lay a large coffee table tome with several pictures of swords and daggers on the front. The Border Patrol officers carried a smallish sword since the drug world loved their blades. Hence the ridiculously sexy, black leather wrist guards the men wore as well to protect their arms from getting sliced up. The leather was reinforced with steel. The female BP officers, of which there were a few, wore them as well.

She set the Egypt book back down and meandered in the direction of a small patio. There was a single Adirondack chair and a nearby table. She had a strong sense of Connor's solitude, otherwise there would have been two chairs or more and a patio table.

He appeared to be as alone as she was.

But she was stunned to find a collection of nicely crafted redwood planters outside, each bearing some kind of succulent or cactus.

As a witch, she knew better than anyone the importance of having and caring for a garden. All kinds of energies moved in and out of the plants and the soil. Even the insects that arrived to partake of the bounty had a purpose and changed things.

Checking to make sure the wood was sanded down smooth, she slowly lowered her bare-ish bottom onto the chair. So far, so good. She sipped more of her wine and tried to figure out what she was seeing. Connor's home looked thought-out, not just jumbled together, another sign he'd been around longer than the thirty-years he looked.

After a few minutes, she went back inside, closing the sliding glass door behind her. A black t-shirt lay on the couch and in the distance, she heard the shower running.

She unclipped her Sig holster and settled it on the nearest sofa cushion. Her belt and jeans were next. After she unbuckled and set the button loose, she unzipped, then slowly slid her pants down her achy body.

Her cuts and bruises were only half healed. If she'd been badly injured, she would have needed some quiet time and a homemade salve made with her favorite medicinal herbs. And a long soak in her tub steeped with bay leaves, lavender, and rosemary.

Sliding off her top, she donned Connor's black t-shirt. It hit her mid-thigh, which would cover her well enough for now. She folded up her clothes and pulled her cell from her pants pocket, grateful not to have lost her phone in the blast. She then gathered up her belongings and placed them in a neat pile on the dining table.

She smelled the sleeve of Connor's shirt, liking how fresh it was. She'd been a witch for ten years and in all that time she'd never been this close to a vampire. She'd long since supposed they all lived like animals. She knew it wasn't universally true, but so many did, lost as a lot of them were to the flame drugs.

She thought about calling for a cab and heading home, but chose to wait. She needed to talk with Connor before she left, even to thank him again.

But as her thoughts turned back to the explosion, once more she pondered why she and Connor had been summoned to Sentinel. Who the hell wanted them dead?

~~ * ~~

After showering, Connor returned to the living room and invited Iris to join him at the dining table. He had a solid reason for not wanting to sit beside her on the couch. Her legs were way too bare and some of his damn fantasies, especially the more involved ones, had taken place on his couch.

He'd done a lot of thinking in the shower. He suspected he'd get some answers from Big Nuts about who or what was behind the set-up.

What he couldn't put together was how he might be connected to a witch he'd never formally met before.

Iris sat down at the table, angling her chair toward him. He leaned his forearms on his thighs, his chair also turned away from the table. The relative position however, gave him another solid view of her shapely legs.

He slid his gaze up, intending to land on her face, but got stuck on her throat. He saw the pulse and a different kind of lust worked him. He'd heard witch blood was the best. He'd had it once, but he'd been lost in blood flame and had no memories of it. Guilt of course tried to rise, but he pushed it down and for a bare moment allowed himself to wonder what Iris's blood would be like flowing down his throat.

This led to other issues, so he finally forced himself to focus on what had led them here together tonight. "What's your job description at the Tribunal? I know you're a Public Safety officer, but what do you do specifically?"

"I work the tip-line and observe crime scenes. Mostly, I make a lot of reports that are usually ignored. Occasionally, I'm sent out to assess an out of control vampire, warlock, witch or shifter. If needed, I'll take him or her out, but always with an eye to public safety."

He nodded. "Sounds like a shit job."

He watched her shoulders fall about a quarter of an inch. He liked that she worked hard not to show her emotions. Of course in Five Bridges, revealing your cards could get you killed.

"You could call it that, except every once in a while I get to do some good." She chuckled softly. "I'd hoped to do some real good tonight and take out a corrupt Border Patrol officer. Then you carried that woman away instead of killing her."

He measured the look in her eye. "You would have done it, too. You would have shot me out there in the wash if I'd killed her."

"Yes, I would have."

He narrowed his gaze. "But I would have had a legal right, decreed by the Tribunal, to kill any runner attempting to take drugs out of Five Bridges."

"But you didn't kill her."

"The point is, if I had, you would have killed me."

She nodded. "But even I could see the woman was thin and very weak. She posed no threat and I'm sure you knew she wasn't likely to succeed in getting the drugs to the border."

"So you could see her? At that distance?"

"My spotting scope could, which means I could see the flame rash on her neck. I knew she was a drug addict and probably desperate. Mostly, I knew you could easily overpower her. So yes, if you'd killed the woman, I would have taken my shot."

For some reason, Connor wasn't bothered at all, probably because he knew Iris as well as he did. And she hadn't shot him though she could have. As a TPS officer, and in the employ of the Five Bridges central government, she had more clout under Tribunal law. It would have been her word against Crescent authority as to what happened.

Witches lied all the time, so he had to give her this: She chose to act on what she actually saw.

He respected her for it.

"I'm sure you've been thinking about what happened on Sentinel Bridge. Have you uncovered a possible connection between us?"

She shook her head. "No, but there must be something we share in common. I'm just not seeing it. I've never actually met you before tonight. I mean I know who you are, and I've seen you dozens of times at various crime scenes, but I don't know any of the Crescent Border Patrol officers."

He nodded, thinking. "And do you usually work near Sentinel Bridge or west Crescent Territory?"

"Rarely. If anything, my assignments involve Savage." The shifters in their province had chosen the right name. Humans who went wolf entered a wild reckless world, more than even vampires. But they tended to fight between packs as opposed to lashing out at witches or vampires. They left the fae and dead-talkers alone as well.

He nodded, but his gaze once more slid over to the exposed parts of her thighs. In response, she crossed her knees. Without warning, his desire for her shot through his skull once more, heating up his groin. His fantasies had been vivid as hell and one of them had involved putting his hands right where one knee rested over the other and easing her legs apart.

He turned away from her and cleared his throat. It would do no good to give his lust free rein right now.

~~ * ~~

Iris's cheeks were warm but it had nothing to do with embarrassment. She'd basically caught Connor lusting after her and despite their strange shared situation, she liked it. Craved it.

She tried to remind herself that he was a vampire, the enemy of her kind. But right now, all she saw was a man, wearing a snug tank, his tats exposed over muscular shoulders and a flat six-pack that had her fingers itching to touch him. He also wore the BP standard issue black leathers, which did not help her craving. He'd settled his sword, wrist guards and Glock on the table next to her own pile.

She put a hand to her chest, aware her heartrate had just spiked. The proximity was killing her and it was time, if possible, to create some physical distance. "I should be getting back to HQ. I need to let Donaldson know I'm still alive."

The permanent line between Connor's brows deepened. "But what if he's part of this, Iris? Everyone knows he's on the take and you already said he requested you. It's possible he was directly involved in the assassination attempt since the Trib has the ability to shut any of the bridges down. If he's involved, he might be under some obligation to send someone else after you."

She rubbed her forehead. "You're right. Someone got to him."

"We need to figure out what's going on here before we split up. And as it happens, I have a lead."

He told her about Gary Smith, who Iris knew was called Big Nuts behind Gary's back. She'd seen him several times and knew exactly why he'd earned the nickname. He had the biggest balls she'd ever seen and for some reason enjoyed showing them off.

He also owned a sex club that featured overweight women called House of Big Sex.

"Why Big Nuts?"

He smiled, probably because she had no problem using Gary's nickname, as horribly descriptive as it was. "Tammy said she owed him for some blood flame. He's the one who sent her out to Amado."

Once more, her gaze moved from Connor's left shoulder to his right. He was a physically powerful man and was probably her best chance of surviving the night, whatever path it took.

When she'd first realized Connor had started visiting her home, hovering above her garden while she worked in it, she'd searched him on the net. She found out he'd worked as an engineer and had built over fifty of the bridges throughout Shadow and Crescent.

She remembered being stunned to learn that a vampire had created anything useful. The fae were the real workers of Five Bridges as well as the dead-talkers. Maybe that was the moment she knew she was in trouble with him.

"Iris, there's one thing I'd like to know. I'm fully aware that most witches wouldn't get this close to a vampire without engaging an enthralling spell. Why haven't you tried one of your witchy trips on me? Tried to control me?"

She rarely talked about these things, about her craft or her philosophy of being a witch. But it seemed appropriate now. "Mostly, I don't believe in it."

"Could you do it, though? Do you have that level of skill and power?"

"I do." A shot of fear went through her. "But please don't tell anyone."

He frowned. "Why not?"

"There are dark forces in Elegance among the various more powerful covens. Witches who practice the dark arts summon power from evil spiritual elements that have taken root in Five Bridges. These women, and a few wizards, don't hesitate to use their gifts to enslave witches of power like me."

He cocked his head. "Is that why you live such a solitary existence?"

"It's definitely the main reason. I have a healthy fear of vampires, but an absolute dread of dark witches."

"Anyone in particular?"

"You've probably heard of her. Seraphina."

His nostrils flared and his lips turned down. "I'd kill her if I could find her."

Seraphina and her group had murdered over a hundred of Connor's kind in the last year alone. Rumors had it she planned one day to rule the Tribunal with the intent of turning Crescent into a police state.

Still looking at her, Connor narrowed his eyes once more, something he did a lot. His eyes were incredibly blue, his brow as furrowed as ever. "I need to be honest here. None of the criminal encounters I've had with witches have ended well. I've destroyed many of your kind and thought nothing of it."

"But my guess is, you only take a life during the commission of a violent crime. Am I right?"

Connor shifted his gaze away from her. His eyes looked haunted. "Not always. There have been a couple of incidences where I was out of control and deserved to be taken out. If you'd seen me, you would have shot me and I would have welcomed it."

This was a lot of honesty and she wasn't sure what to do with the information. Finally, she said, "Did these events happen earlier in your life?"

"Somewhat. Yes." He shifted his gaze to stare at the slate floor. "And they're my biggest regrets."

Iris could have pressed him for more details, but she didn't want to know too much. If he told her, she was pretty sure she'd have to leave. And right now, she needed him.

"I'm not innocent either. When my sister, Violet, was murdered, I'd fully intended on hunting down the vampires who tortured, raped and killed her. If I'd found them, I know I would have used any witch power I possessed to drive them into the dirt."

"Iris, I'm really sorry you lost your sister. You never discovered who did it?"

"No."

"Can you tell me when this happened?"

"I'd rather not go into it. I've worked hard over the years to let it go. Had to, otherwise I was slowly going insane. But I miss her."

"I understand."

She considered him for a moment. "Have you ever killed a vampire?" She knew what she was doing; she was looking for some reason to dislike Connor. The proximity of the situation was beating her down and giving rise to a lot of unhelpful ideas. If he confessed to showing partiality to his own species, she could think badly of him and maybe then she wouldn't crave him the way she did.

Mostly, he sat so close she had to keep resisting a powerful urge to touch him and to glide her hand over his massive shoulders.

God help her, was she falling for a vampire?

~~ * ~~

Connor felt weighed down by the conversation. He hated sharing the nature of his actions and the why's of anything he did. Yet he felt a strong need to as honest with Iris as much as he could. "I have a lot of guilt over some of the vampires I've taken out. But each time, I'd caught them in the middle of a violent crime. I'm sure my answer isn't what you expected, but, yes, I kill my kind as well."

She shook her head, eyes wide. "I've never met an officer like you. Most of the Crescent Border Patrol spit at me and refuse to share details about a scene I've been sent to report on. And since we're being honest, I thought all of you were corrupt. That's the word on the street that no officer is beyond being bought off."

He hated the stereotype. "Not me. Not some of my brothers, though maybe half the force is greasing its fingers."

"But not you?"

"Did you need to ask twice?"

She shook her head and released a whistling sound through her lips. "No. I apologize."

She shouldn't be so pretty. That's what he thought. She had large brown eyes that glinted when she was mad. He'd like to see those same eyes lit with passion.

He knew she was interested. She might even need a good lay, especially someone like her who seemed to go it alone. They were alike in that way. He'd been checking up on her for months and in all that time she'd never gone out on a single date.

His gaze fell to her fingers. She had beautiful hands, the nails trimmed close and covered with some kind of shimmering violet polish. But he had to remind himself that with enough power, she could release a killing shot from the tip of one of those fingers. If she felt justified in doing it, she'd kill him without batting an eye.

He'd be smart to keep his distance, but the proximity tonight had doubled his desire for her. The whole time they'd been talking, he was hiding an erection. What was it about Iris that got to him so completely?

"I'm going to need a change of clothes," she said. "And a quick shower. Also, you might want to bring some fresh gear with you to my house."

"Why?" The thought of needing to put on a different set of clothes for any reason, had his groin humming once more.

"Call it an instinct, though it's closer to prescience this time. Trust me, you'll need some of your things at my house."

"All right. I'll take your word for it."

She sighed. "But after that, where do we find Big Nuts this time of night?"

CHAPTER THREE

A few minutes later, Iris had her arms pinned around Connor's neck as he flew her through the air. With his arm tight around her waist and her feet balanced on his boot, the t-shirt was drawn up to the bottom of her buttocks. To anyone below, she would have been fully exposed. But Connor had taken them to an even higher altitude than before. This meant, of course, that she was frightened half out of her wits and worked hard to keep from repeating her strangling technique.

Yet at the same time, desire flowed through her once more. Her breasts were flat up against Connor's muscled chest and as he maneuvered through the air, his pecs would tighten and release, teasing her badly. Each time, she had to repress a moan of pure pleasure. It had been a long time since she'd been with a man. She'd had a few casual relationships since her *alter*, but nothing significant.

She'd been married for two years when she entered Five Bridges with her sister. She'd lost so much because of the *alter*, something she tried not to think about very often. Grief was never a simple process and hers, because she'd had to leave a husband she loved behind, was still a decade old, still hurt, and might always be an ache in her heart.

Even worse, she'd been pregnant at the time and the *alter* had taken the life of her little girl.

But holding onto Connor in such a tight embrace reminded her how good life could be. In this moment, she could set everything aside and remember what it had been like to desire someone like mad, to want to be only with him, to need to share his bed.

41

He slowed down as he passed over Sentinel Bridge. "Take a look, Iris. I know flying unsettles you, but you won't believe what I'm seeing. I think your bike is still intact. And don't worry, I have you."

She hadn't planned on releasing her iron grip on his shoulders and neck, but the mention of her Trib cruiser had her easing back. When she'd made enough space to see, she looked down. At the same time, Connor slowed in the air.

The first thing she saw was a pit on the bridge about fifteen feet wide. But Connor had been right, her bike was still there, a good ten feet from the edge of the hole. Rubble was everywhere.

Not surprising, though the bombed-out section was cordoned off, several TPS officers directed traffic around the gaping hole. The reality was simple; the drug lords only made money if humans kept moving through Five Bridges and spending their weekly earnings.

"You're body's grown stiff, Iris. You mad?"

"It seems so disrespectful to Jason and Sadie. Couldn't the bridge stay closed for five minutes?"

"You know what our world is."

She sighed and when he began picking up speed, she once more wrapped her arms securely around his neck. "I know, but it really bugs me."

"I hear you."

Connor zipped her through the air back to Elegance. At least she didn't have to give him directions, a thought that made her chuckle. Was it only a couple of hours ago that she'd looked up into the night sky, hunting for him?

"Something funny?"

"I'm not sure. It's hard to know how to react to all we've been through, and the night's not over yet." Absently, she ran a finger along the short shoulder seam of his tank. The hilt of his sword was pressed into her right hip and she could feel his Glock against her left.

Connor had given her a canvas bag for her belongings, which he now carried in his free hand along with his own travel bag slung over his shoulder. The man was thoughtful.

When he began his descent toward her house, she suggested he land in the backyard. "I'd rather my neighbors didn't see us on the front porch."

"Good idea."

Slowly, he eased past the huge tree to the small patch of lawn she kept in the middle of her jungle-like garden.

Once she stepped off his boot, she took the canvas bag from his hand, then told him to make himself at home. She headed inside, but left the French doors wide to make sure Connor knew he was welcome to come in.

She went to her bedroom and after closing the door, she planted a hand between her breasts. She could feel her heart pounding. What was it about Connor that ramped her up so completely?

She needed some help calming down. She crossed to the bedside table and lit the small candle beneath a miniature cauldron. The flame would be enough to warm up the water and send lavender streaming through the air. For her, nothing eased her like this fragrance.

The room quickly filled with the edgy floral scent. From her chest of drawers, she withdrew a packet of bay leaves. Taking a small one out, she slipped it under her tongue. Bay had a protective effect and would also support her present need for wisdom. She couldn't keep the leaf in place for very long, however, or she would easily slide into a vision-state.

She removed Connor's shirt, folded it up and set it outside her bedroom door. She'd almost thrown it on the bed, which would have been nothing short of a witchy invitation for the man to hurry in here and take possession of her body.

The same earlier sensation returned of craving Connor desperately. She almost retrieved his shirt from the hall. After all, would it really be so bad to make use of his incredibly muscular body?

When her mind began to swirl faintly, she plucked the bay leaf from her mouth, crossed to the brew pot and laid it on top of the small lavender flowers and stems.

Time to get cleaned up. She slid into a robe, gathered up a fresh set of clothes and crossed the hall to the bathroom, the only one in her small house.

Once in the shower, she dipped beneath the spray.

Nothing could have felt better than the stream of hot water hitting her neck and shoulders. She washed her hair as well since the explosion had given her an odd metallic smell.

She'd always found showers a cleansing experience on more than one level. Given what she'd just been through, she spoke a series of incantations to purify her soul, her body and her home from all bad influences. She thought perhaps in this way, her desire for Connor might be eased as well.

When she finally shut the shower off, a new wind blew through the bathroom, smelling of thyme again.

"Violet, you're here?" She was surprised to have another visit. In all this time, she might have felt her sister's presence on occasion, but never with this level of connection which also involved telepathy.

Yes, I'm here, Iris. A sense of urgency accompanied her words.

"I can feel that you're distressed. What's wrong? Is there something you need me to do?"

Save Connor.

She wondered if she'd heard right. "You want me to save Connor?"

Yes.

Iris would have asked what she meant, but just like that, the wind swept from the room and Violet was gone.

Iris stood very still for a long time processing the strange conversation. But it made no sense. Why did Connor need saving?

~~ * ~~

Deep in the garden, Connor stared up at the owl named Sebastien. He was a sturdy-looking, beige and brown predator bird and sat on one of several large branches of a massive sissoo tree. As a forest creature, he was way out of his element in the desert, yet he looked at home in Iris's garden.

Connor had never been in a witch's dwelling before and what he'd seen earlier had stunned him. Plants grew everywhere within her home, in dozens of pots and containers, many of them creeping over trellises and latticework attached to the walls. A yellow cat had sat near the legs of the dining table, watching him as he moved around the small rooms. Her house might be a detached home, but it wasn't much bigger than his townhouse.

And here in the garden, he felt as though the plants were all leaning toward him and trying to talk to him. It was odd, yet pleasant in a way he couldn't explain.

He was definitely in Elegance.

"Everything okay?"

He heard Iris's voice and turned toward her. At the same moment, a wind suddenly hit him in the back. He even lurched forward a couple of steps.

The same gust flowed in Iris's direction. When it reached her, she held out both hands and closed her eyes, savoring whatever this was.

A few seconds later, the night was once more very still. "What was that?"

"Violet, my deceased sister. She's been active tonight, though I'm not sure why. I think she's worried about me."

As she moved onto the patio near what appeared to be a small workroom on the right, she stopped near a tall lattice of blooming, purple flowers. He watched the flowers sway in her direction. It was like seeing music take physical shape. The cat crossed the threshold behind her. The owl hooted.

Iris looked beautiful. Her hair was damp from her shower, and she wore it in the usual ponytail, which in turn framed her lovely features. She had angled cheekbones, a creamy complexion and full lips. She wore another snug, short-sleeved t-shirt, jeans and a pair of sturdy running shoes.

A calm came over him. A decision made. He knew exactly what he was going to do, what he'd been wanting to do for a long time. The time and place were right. After all, he was in Iris's garden.

He unclipped his holster and the sword sheath, setting his weapons on the grass, then held out his hand to her. What needed to happen had to be with the approval of her owl, as well as the yellow cat now rubbing around her ankles.

She looked serious as she began walking toward him, her eyes wide. A soft flow of energy moved from plant to plant, following her as she took each step. He felt it all and it only increased his need for her.

"Connor?" She stood a couple of polite feet away. Her gaze flipped over his Glock and his sword, then back to him.

"I love your garden," he said quietly. He glanced down at the cat, who sat and stared up at him. Approval? He looked up at the owl, who appeared to dip his head. Definitely approval.

He closed the distance and drew Iris into his arms.

He heard her gasp faintly. Would she reject him? Struggle against him?

He felt a tension in her, but he kissed her anyway, a firm demanding kiss. He teased the seam of her lips with his tongue, but she didn't part for him.

A moment passed, then another and her tension remained. Yet still he kissed her.

When she didn't respond, he finally drew back.

Her eyes were still wide, but she didn't move away from him.

Had he offended her? Had he misunderstood the signs? Wasn't she interested?

But her gaze fell to his lips and she uttered a soft, almost anguished cry. Then she was on him, her arms wrapped around his neck, almost as desperately as when she'd flown through the air with him. She kissed him fiercely, his lips, his cheeks, his chin. He'd never experienced anything like it.

All his concern fled, and he tightened his arms around her so he could feel the full length of her. He returned her kiss, dragging his tongue over her lips once more. When she opened for him, he uttered a heavy groan and drove inside.

How many times had he imagined being right here, in her garden, the woman in his arms. His doubts that she might not have the same need melted away. He gave himself to the kiss, his cock already hard and ready, his hands sliding over her back then her bottom, caressing her.

It would take so little to bring her the rest of the way. She was as ready for him as he was anxious to enter her body. It became his mission to bring her to a roaring orgasm.

But after a moment, when the initial wave passed, he released her just enough to meet her gaze. "I've wanted to do that for months now, ever since I saw you at the Tribunal comforting that woman."

"Which woman?"

"I have no idea. But I've been hooked since."

She rested her arms on his shoulders. "I want to be with you Connor. I do. Even though you're a vampire. You've proven yourself in so many ways. You have a good, decent heart."

His turn to dip his chin. "That's part of it, isn't it? Because I value who you are as well, even though you're a species I despise."

"Exactly."

No recriminations. They'd both lived in the world long enough to accept what each was. "But we have a job to do right now."

She nodded.

He didn't want to let go of her. He was afraid if he did, he'd never find his way back to this moment. And somehow, making love to her had become a critical part of his future, his life.

She released him. "Let me get my Sig." She moved back into the house, returning with her sidearm clipped to her belt. "Gary's place is still in Rotten Row, right?"

"Yep. And the Row has gotten worse in recent years. Just wanted you to know."

"Then it's a good thing I'm allowed to carry a gun."

He offered her a half-smile. "You might get to kill some vampires tonight."

"In the line of duty, I have no problem taking out bad guys, no matter what species. And don't let my looks fool you. I'm not squeamish. Plus, I can use my killing power to bring down just about anyone, if needed."

Connor repressed a sigh. She'd just reminded him why he should be keeping his distance.

An odd expression crossed her face and her gaze drifted up into the night sky. "Connor, we're not alone."

Connor picked up his holster from off the grass and drew his Glock into his hand. He bent his knees and tilted his head to also look up into the sky.

Christ, what now?

~~ * ~~

Iris could feel the vampire hovering but saw nothing in the dark sky. She drew close to Connor, his sudden intensity like a wave of heat flowing over her.

Vampires could partially disguise themselves from her kind, but she wondered if Connor would be able to get a visual of a fellow creature. "Do you see anything?"

"No," he said quietly. "But you're right. He's there."

A moment later, the sensation passed. She always knew when Connor left and it was the same now with this new intruder. "He's gone, isn't he?"

"Yep. He took off." She watched Connor clip his holster back on his belt then slide the gun inside.

"Who do you think it was? Were we followed?"

Connor shook his head. "I haven't a clue on either count. But he was probably connected to all the other events tonight."

"I have an idea." She put her hand on his chest. "Take me into the air right now. I want to try something."

"Is this a witch thing?"

She nodded. "Yes. You okay with that?"

He offered a half-smile. "With you, I am."

Iris's heart swelled, loving that he trusted her.

Connor moved her to his left side, then lifted her onto his boot. When she had one arm wrapped around his neck, he drew her tight against his side. "Do you feel secure like this?"

She ignored her racing heart. "I'll get used to it."

With his right hand, he palmed his Glock once more, then rose slowly into the air. "Let me know what you want me to do."

She put her free hand on his chest for balance, but forced herself to watch her garden recede. "Keep going," she murmured. "Higher, until I tell you to stop."

She said nothing more for thirty feet, then forty. But another few yards and she could feel the disturbed quality of the air. He must have felt it as well because he halted at about the same time she told him they'd gone far enough.

"You feel it too?" she whispered.

"I do."

She closed her eyes and focused on all the sensations still floating in the air. After a few seconds, she shivered.

"What?"

"I feel him, Connor. Though he's gone, he's left behind a sense of himself. He's very dark and angry and there seems to be a kind of madness in him. And he's powerful. But there's something more. He feels familiar to me. Someone I met, but not recently. I just can't quite figure out who."

A moment later, she shook her head. "It's gone. You can take me back to the garden. Also, there's something critical I feel I must do before we leave."

Connor lowered her swiftly.

Once on solid ground, she went into her workroom where earlier she had almost employed a spell to get rid of her desire for Connor. Her efforts this time, however, had nothing to do with him.

Using pestle and mortar, she quickly pulverized the resin of dragon's blood into a powder. When she had a sufficient quantity, she moved into the house then headed straight to the front door. Bending down, she spread a thin line next to the entire threshold for security.

She did the same at the French doors that opened onto her garden. Her plants swayed and moved with her as she silently invoked an incantation of protection. Not in all her years in Five Bridges had she felt the need to shield her home.

Then she'd been called to Amado Bridge and everything had changed.

She spread a final line inside her bedroom French doors and felt the protection lock into place.

When she turned toward Connor, she saw that he watched her with a concerned frown pulling his brows together. "What did you just do? Because I felt as though your garden was ready to start a riot."

She explained about the spell. "I've just never had to worry before. Connor, what's happening here? I don't know what I've done to have brought this down on my head."

Connor drew close. "That's what we need to find out and remember, you're not alone here. I'm in this as much as you are."

"Right. Well, then we need to get to Rotten Row and see what Big Nuts has to say."

Connor was a fast flyer, which indicated his basic power level as a vampire as well as his age.

His path led him on a northwesterly course back into Crescent Territory closer to Amado Bridge than to his home at the east end. She never traveled to Rotten Row on her own and the Tribunal had refused to send TPS officers to any of the crime scenes located in that area of Crescent.

Rotten Row was run by several gangster types, each into drug-running, human trafficking and prostitution. The three main drug-lords had numerous establishments there as well.

She felt Connor slow his speed, though he remained at least forty feet up in the air. She realized she'd gained confidence in his flying ability and was able to look down all the time now.

Gaudy lights flashed from nearly every venue down a street that extended a full four miles. A variety of music pulsed in the air, most of it loud. Hundreds of young women, a good number of them human and dressed in next to nothing, strolled the sidewalk.

Cars cruised, pulling over often. Women would get in and maybe they'd never be seen again. Or they'd be dumped in No Man's Land, a desolate place in the middle of Five Bridges also called the Graveyard. None of the five species lived in that pitted, barren area.

"You keep sighing."

"I do? I hadn't realized I was. But this is so hard to take, this part of our world. Sometimes I wonder if we'll ever make progress."

"I know what you mean." Connor cruised at a slow pace now, but still well above the lights.

"Did you know that when the Tribunal clean-up squads go out to the Graveyard at dawn, they cart off as many as twenty bodies every night, most of them women? And oftentimes a couple of them aren't even dead."

"I know. We've got a tragedy on our hands."

Early on, before becoming a TPS officer, she'd gotten a job at the Tribunal. She'd been assigned to the missing persons desk. Residents of Phoenix would call to report that a loved one had disappeared and her job would be to locate them if possible, which was rarely.

There'd been one case that had shredded her heart. She'd worked with a young husband named Evan, who'd been a talented tax accountant for a powerful Paradise Valley mover-and-shaker. Evan had gone to a Christmas party with his pregnant wife, Heather, and from that expensive home, she'd had been abducted.

Evan had called the Tribunal, desperate to find his wife. With a Trib passport, Iris had left Five Bridges to meet Evan at his Phoenix home so that she could get a picture of Heather as well as to take some personal things with her to be used in casting a spell.

For the first few weeks, she'd made progress, and her spell seemed to be having a strong effect. She would locate someone who had seen

Heather and who was willing to talk. She'd gain some information then learn of another person who would share with her as well.

Evan called several times a night for a progress report. The Tribunal wouldn't allow him to search for his wife on his own because of the risk the cartels posed to his own life if he started asking questions. Iris knew he was frantic with worry.

She followed up quickly on each lead. She'd been able to confirm that Heather had been taken into Five Bridges, specifically into Crescent Territory. She was being used as a prostitute, which was terrible all on its own. But Iris had known it was the best possible news because Heather hadn't been given an *alter* serum, which meant she was alive and still human. Her captors, however, were keeping her strung out on blood flame and the drug would be hard on her baby.

Iris had kept nothing back from Evan. She'd been up front from the beginning, especially about his wife's odds of survival as well as the child she carried.

At the two-month mark, however, when her investigation led her way-too-close to one of the drug-lords, Donaldson had told her to close the file.

Iris had begged to be allowed to continue. She'd been so hopeful of a positive outcome. But Donaldson had insisted; she wasn't to spend another second on Heather's case.

One of the hardest things she'd ever done was to pay Evan a final visit. She'd wept when she told him that her superior had shut the investigation down.

Evan had grown very calm and Iris knew he'd begun the process of acceptance, that he would probably never see his wife again.

A week later, Iris had received a report that included a picture of a very pregnant woman shot down in a drug raid. She knew at once the woman was Evan's wife since she had a photo of her. Besides, every witch instinct she had told Iris who the woman was. For whatever reason, Heather's captors had decided to use her to run drugs.

Evan had confirmed the woman's identity. He'd taken Heather back to Phoenix, buried his wife and their unborn son, and she'd never seen him again.

But the way Evan had been so desperate to recover Heather during those early days and weeks now burned as Iris's prime motivation. Somehow, she would be part of the process, no matter how long it took, to create a decent society within Five Bridges.

Her own unfortunate path to becoming an *alter* witch might not have been something she'd asked for. But she'd come to accept her fate and intended to make the most of it.

Even if it meant heading into the worst part of Crescent, into a place known as home to several death squads.

~~ * ~~

A few minutes later, Connor descended in stages down to the street, though he remained levitating. The noise was almost deafening from the constant honking of cars, to women shouting and music exploding from one establishment to the next.

Several vampires were in the air, levitating in a drunk way. One of them slammed into the running lights of a one-hour hotel, sending sparks flashing as he tumbled to the sidewalk. Hard.

"Oh, dear God," Iris murmured.

Connor followed the line of Iris's sight and saw why she sounded distressed. The vampire's skull had cracked open and blood poured onto the cement.

He turned her away from the carnage, levitated above the traffic and flew across to the entrance of the House of Big Sex. A red sign flashed steadily, 'Big-Women-All-the-Time'.

Connor knew better than to try to enter the establishment once he touched down on concrete. He slowly moved Iris off his boot, but kept his arm around her waist, holding her tight.

He hadn't discussed strategy with her, which meant on some level he trusted her instincts to go with the flow. He knew she'd been a TPS officer for over nine years and he relied on her experience to help see this encounter with Gary through.

Big Nuts had some of the meanest shifter bouncers and bodyguards of anyone on the Row. Two of them approached him now, mouths in tight, grim lines, eyes small and feral, noses sniffing the air. Very shifter.

He addressed the taller one, meeting his gaze dead on. "Alejandro. We need to see your boss." He knew by long habit how to read the hierarchy among the fur-beasts and Alejandro, with the sides of his head shaved clean and heavy tattoos running from his scalp down the sides of his neck, was an alpha.

He ran Gary's entire security force.

Alejandro met his gaze, nostrils flaring as he swept his dark, beady eyes to Iris. "No fucking witches allowed. Bosses orders."

"He'll want to see this one. She knew the bridge would blow and we're both alive because of it."

Connor had a decent working relationship with Big Nuts, primarily because Gary only accepted willing workers and never killed them off. Of course, by the time each came to him, they were strung out on flame, which made it easy to control the women who worked for him.

Alejandro shifted his gaze several times between the two of them. He didn't look convinced and gestured for his partner to form a barrier between Connor and the door. He disappeared inside for a moment.

When he reappeared, he signaled for them to follow.

"Here we go," he whispered to Iris.

To her credit, Iris moved right with him, not hesitating once, though he did notice she kept her palm on the butt of her Sig.

Once inside, he slowed his pace, needing a moment to adjust. The women in Big Nuts's stable were all large women, some even super-sized with narrow strips of silk tucked between erotic rolls. Several were actively engaged in a variety of sex acts with various patrons. The club hummed, moaned, and screamed with activity.

"Do you see that?" Iris whispered. She was doing a good job of keeping pace with him since Alejandro was moving fast across the expansive club, heading to the hallway beyond.

"You mean the women?" Was she referring to the obvious? Or was it something else?

"Several of them are pregnant."

He took a couple of seconds to do a deeper search of the room and she was right. Not only were there large women serving the clientele but several average-sized women who were with child.

He'd only been inside Gary's club a few times, but he'd never noticed pregnant women before. Of course, he hadn't been looking, either. Connor's work was centered on drug-running, not sex-for-sale enterprises. Any business he'd had with Big Nuts would have involved seeking information about a runner.

~~ * ~~

Iris tried to ignore the smells assaulting her from within the oh-so-fine establishment. She smelled sex and a variety of body odors, a cigar stench and somewhere a layering of beer and vomit.

Having reached the opposite side of the room and passed down a narrow hall, Alejandro stood outside a doorway. Two plump, naked beauties held back a pair of blue velvet curtains. Iris half-expected Big Nuts to be reclining on pillows with several women servicing him.

Instead, he sat behind a desk, smoking a cigar, his eyes narrowed as if in some discomfort. Four bodyguards, in addition to Alejandro, were stationed around the room.

She forced herself to take deep breaths, not because she was frightened, but because the wood-paneling of the room was trying to talk to her, screaming at her.

Violence was part of night-life in the Row. So of course the organic elements of the room would try to gain her attention, to warn her away. She even thought about attempting a calming spell. But she knew the moment she lit up her witch skills, one of the vampires present would probably cut her throat.

Big Nuts looked her up and down. He was bald, had a wide nose, and wore a black tank like Connor that showcased his shoulder tattoos, one of them a screaming skull. "You're pretty for a witch. Too skinny, though." As an *alter* species, he could tell she was a witch just as she knew he was a vampire.

He rose from his chair, then rounded the desk to plant his ass on the corner, legs wide. He wore snug, leopard print pants.

Okay, she couldn't help herself. Her gaze dropped to the bulge across his groin and there they were, about the size of softballs, which was probably the most accurate description possible in every respect. There was nothing sexy in the display, however. Rather, she felt like she was standing next to a cage at the zoo, looking at an animal she'd never seen before.

Gary's nickname suited him extremely well.

When she could finally lift her gaze to his face, he wore a satisfied smile and took a drag on his fat cigar. It was as though God had given him a single outstanding asset and he worked it like a one-ring circus.

"So you knew the bridge would blow. That a witch thing?"

"*My* witch thing. Yes."

"Yeah, you witches have a complete panorama of gifts. I lose track. And I never use one of your kind in my club, in case you're offering."

"I'm not."

Big Nuts's gaze slid to Connor. "What d'you want, anyway, Officer?"

Connor's deep voice rolled through the room. "Heard a rumor you sent a runner my way tonight. A woman with a fake jacket. I need to know why."

Iris felt the tenor of the room change, like a first strike of lightning in a thunder storm. It was a warning from a spiritual plane and she knew she couldn't ignore it.

She drew her gun, whirled, then settled her back against Connor's arm. She was essentially at a right-angle to him. He didn't move, yet she could feel his body had drawn up into a single tense line, ready for action as well.

Big Nuts's bodyguard force came to attention during the same split-second of movement. Blades came out and a couple of hand guns.

"Back-off," Iris cried out, "or I'll start shooting because I don't give a damn who dies here tonight. Not me, not Connor, not any of you."

There was a joint intake of breath. A few of the bodyguards muttered a string of expletives. A witch making threats in a Crescent Territory establishment was something to be feared.

Gary waved a hand. "Put your weapons away."

Big Nuts's force obeyed immediately, though all eyes were on her.

"What are you doing?" Connor asked, nudging her gently with his arm from behind.

"Protecting your ass."

For some reason, this made Connor chuckle. "Thanks, but I got this."

"You sure? Because I felt a premonition glide through the room. I think maybe you need to ask Big Nuts here who paid him to set you up?" Iris didn't shift position. The warning still registered with her like an itch on her skin. She kept her gaze moving from the shifters she could see back to the velvet curtains and the two women ready to reopen them on command. Each stood with eyes wide and panicked.

Connor's voice once more rolled through the space. "So, Gary, why did you set me up?"

"It was all in fun. I sent Tammy out there myself just to give you a hard time. No one else had a hand in it. This is on me."

Iris didn't hesitate to share her thoughts. "He's lying."

~~ * ~~

Connor loved that Iris was as deeply engaged in the process as he was and he could feel her witchness as she stayed connected to his arm. She'd also brought the real issue to the forefront, exactly where it needed to be.

He began again, holding Gary's gaze tight. "Now, why do you want to lie to me? Haven't I always been fair with you? When was the last time I raided your establishment?"

"Never."

"Exactly. So, why the runner?"

Big Nuts released a heavy sigh. "All right. Someone wanted you to kill her. He was sure you would. Said you had a habit of putting innocent women in the grave."

Clearly, whoever was after him knew the worst parts of his history.

"And how did you know Tammy? She was too thin to be one of your big women."

"She came to me pregnant and knew I hired a few women who could sport the belly. She did good for a while but she pounded down blood flame like you wouldn't believe and I had to let her go. When I was approached with a boatload of cash, I knew Tammy would do whatever I asked. I was right."

Connor grew uneasy, though he wasn't sure why. Something in the room didn't feel right to him either and not because Iris was feeling it. But he couldn't put his finger on the problem.

Then it hit him. There was a theme going on here. The woman he'd killed all those years ago had been pregnant. Tammy had been as well. And Big Nuts used pregnant women as part of his sex club. But none of this would get him the answers he needed.

Yet, as he recalled the woman he'd killed a decade past, guilt drove a spike through his heart all over again. The moment he'd realized the pistol had been strapped to her wrist, he knew he'd been set up, maneuvered to kill the woman. But he'd never known why, never gotten to the bottom of it. Even back then he couldn't find anyone willing to talk.

The event had changed him, made him cautious, more careful than he'd ever been before.

Now here he was, facing a low-level sex club owner who had sent Tammy out to repeat history. "I need to know who set me up. That's all. Then I'm out of here."

He felt Iris tense up once more. "We should leave," she said quietly.

He took in the field once more. Five shifter bodyguards and Big

Nuts. Two women by the blue velvet drapes. Iris's gun and her witch powers, his own weapon still in its holster. His sword at the ready.

He made his move and brought his gun into his hand. He was fast and even Big Nuts's eyes widened.

Big Nuts held up both hands. "Let's calm down."

"Let's not. Iris, start making your way to the door. Gary, you should let us go."

"See, it's this way. I can't. I was told to hold you and these were orders I couldn't refuse."

"Whose orders?"

"Can't tell you that either, except to say it wasn't one of the big three." He lifted both arms in the air and with his index and middle fingers pressed together, waved to his troops. It was a signal of some kind.

Connor fired up into the air and the women at the velvet curtains screamed and ran out of the room. The bodyguards, however, froze in mid-motion like playing statue, but he wasn't sure why. Gary with them.

Then he felt Iris's witch energy all around him, though how she was doing it he had no idea. She seemed to be employing some form of enthrallment, a spell maybe. It was on a massive scale, something most witches couldn't do. So who was Iris anyway?

Connor kept shifting his gaze from Big Nuts, to his men, and back.

"Iris?" He didn't dare take his eyes off the men in front of him, though he feared more guards may have already arrived at the entrance. If they had, he and Iris were screwed.

Connor waited, then asked, "What's going on, Iris?"

She didn't respond, but he could still feel her streaming some kind of spell. And since Big Nuts hadn't moved because he, too, was frozen in place, Connor turned toward the door. But no one was there. No one had come to support Gary's troops.

He then looked back at Iris. Holy shit. She stood eyes closed, with her arms raised, her gun in hand and the pistol pointed toward the ceiling.

He finally understood. She was holding the room in some kind of stasis. All with her own power. Unbelievable.

But it was a brilliant move because he knew exactly how he could make this work for him.

He moved back to Big Nuts, whose eyes looked dull.

"Iris, it would help if you could partially release Gary."

He felt her focusing intently and after a moment, Big Nuts finally blinked, meeting Connor's gaze.

"Tell me now, Gary, who set me up and what species was he?"

Big Nuts shook his head. Despite the fact that his troops were immobilized and couldn't come to his aid, he still wouldn't give up the information.

Connor looked down at the man's leopard pants and the two oversized bulges. How bad would it hurt if he was in a witch-trance?

Time to find out.

Using the butt of his gun, he came down on the left testicle.

Big Nuts arched his neck, opened his mouth wide and a high-pitched scream left his voice.

"Tell me now, Gary, or I'll do the same to the other one."

"He was a vampire but didn't give me his name." Gary's face had turned bright red from pain. He also had a hard time pushing his words out of his throat. "He gave me cash. A lot of it. Seemed like a small thing to do, sending you out to Amado, then over to Sentinel. I didn't know he meant to blow the bridge."

"What did he look like?"

"Couldn't see his face, only his eyes." He squeezed each word out. He was having a hard time breathing. "Green, maybe hazel. Not sure. Black hair. Tall. Lean. But he was in shadow, like some kind of spell was on him. That's all I know."

"You called him, didn't you? Before we came in."

"Yes, he's on his way. A couple minutes out."

"Was he paying you more to turn us over?"

Big Nuts nodded. "A lot. The man has money."

So they were dealing with a vampire of wealth, maybe the vampire who'd shown up at Iris's just before they left.

"I should kill you for this."

Big Nuts glanced down at his crotch. "I think you already did."

Connor was pissed as hell. He brought the butt down on the other ball and watched as Big Nuts folded up then slid off the desk.

He returned to Iris, facing her. "Can you talk while you're holding this spell?"

She shook her head, her eyes still closed.

"Can I?"

She nodded in quick bobs of her chin.

"Good. I want to wait for our mystery man to arrive. You okay with that?"

She shook her head.

"You're running out of steam?"

Another nod.

He noticed the white, compressed look to her lips. "Okay. Can you move?"

Once more, her head wagged side-to-side.

"Can I pick you up?"

She dipped her chin.

He slipped behind her and put her in flight position on his boot once more, holding her close. He levitated slowly back into the hall. He could feel her spell still flooding the space around them.

When he moved into the main sex room, he saw that the spell had shut everyone down there as well. He'd never been more grateful in his life. Or astonished. Iris had a helluva lot of power.

As he moved through the room, he searched for the man who was hunting them, but saw no one who might fit the description.

However, when he slipped through the front door and past the bodyguards, he happened to glance back over his shoulder. A tall vampire with unusually pale skin, stood watching him. He was lean with maybe greenish eyes and had black hair, but that's all Connor could make out. Big Nuts was right; a witch spell of some kind cloaked him. Great. They were dealing with a vampire who didn't mind making use of a witch's powers.

He could feel Iris's spell start to weaken. He rose swiftly into the air and Iris collapsed against him, the spell vanishing at the same moment. He carried her two streets over, then landed to put both guns away. It was tricky since she was limp against him, almost unconscious.

As soon as the weapons were back in each holster, he slid an arm beneath her knees and cradled her against his chest. He then launched back into the air. He realized now that Iris, acting on her prescience, had gotten them both out of there alive, though he didn't know how. For one thing, he should have fallen under the spell at the same time as the others. For another, he'd never heard of a witch being able to enthrall so many at once. Again, Iris must have a phenomenal level of ability.

He decided it would be best to return to her home since she would need time to recover. He knew enough about her culture to understand Iris would gain strength from her garden. But he wasn't sure they should stay there long since their shared enemy knew where she lived.

He flew to her backyard and slowly made his descent. When he touched down on the lawn he looked up and saw that her earlier spell, full of power, had created a shield over her entire property, something that looked like soft trails of mist through the air.

"I can see your spell," he said quietly. He didn't let her go. He knew she'd crumple if he did.

"Makes sense." She spoke slowly, as though drugged. "I included you in the binding incantation. Sorry I'm so weak. I used everything … I had to hold the spell. I knew he wouldn't tell us anything otherwise."

Connor carried her to the back door and opened it carefully. At the same time, the yellow cat rushed out, his quiet bell jingling at his neck.

"Don't take me into the house," she whispered. "Follow Pips."

He turned and saw that the cat was sitting in the middle of the patch of grass, his back to Connor. Pips then turned slightly to watch Connor over his shoulder as though waiting for Connor to figure things out.

When Connor levitated and moved in the cat's direction, Pips trotted to the tree then sat down off to the right of it. "Pips is by the sissoo."

"Take me there. He always knows best." Ah, yes, the world of the witch.

Once he reached the old, massive tree, he had to set her on her feet for a moment, but held her pressed against him. He unclipped his Glock holster first, then his sword, bending to place each on the ground. He picked her up again and leaning against the tree slid down to sit on the grass at the base. He held Iris on his lap, still holding her close.

The tree felt like life to him, as though everything good and powerful in the universe had gathered in one place and showered a life-force down on them both.

A breeze blew through the garden, rustling the leaves of the sissoo, and making a shushing sound.

His throat grew tight and he had the strangest feeling as though for a brief moment he'd returned to the human world restored. He rubbed his gums, checking for the lumps that would release his fangs, but they were still there. The sensation, as transient as it would no doubt prove, made him long for things he'd pushed to the deepest parts of his mind.

He'd been twenty-eight when he'd taken the blood flame drug, laced as it was with the vampire *alter* serum. But in this moment, with Iris in his arms, he could recall the vision he'd had for his life. He would become an engineer and build entire cities. He would find the right woman to be by his side, they would marry and have four or five kids.

He'd found the right woman, but after a year of marriage she'd died unexpectedly of a brain aneurism. His grief had been profound and had led him to take blood flame, which in turn had brought him here, to this exact spot, beneath a life-giving tree and holding a beautiful, strong, resourceful witch in his arms.

When Iris began drawing deep breaths, he felt her strength returning. With skin like cream, her brows in fine arches, and her lips full, she looked like a model.

Without thinking, he stroked her face, pushing a few loose strands away from her ear.

She drew another stream of air into her lungs, then rolled her head back to look up at him. Her gaze skated past him as she looked in the direction of the sky. She smiled. "I'm so glad to be home and you're right, my spell holds. We'll be safe here. I knew you were worried about that."

Her cat jumped up on Iris's stomach. "Hello, Pips."

Iris shifted just enough to pet her cat.

Connor's throat now ached like he had a noose around his neck. For a moment, he didn't know why until he realized he'd felt this way once before, during his way-too-brief marriage.

The night had already been strange with the runner and her fake jacket, the explosion on the bridge, and now Big Nuts turning him over to a madman for cash.

But maybe the most bizarre part was realizing he was falling in love with Iris Meldeere, a woman who by nature of her *alter* species was his enemy.

How the hell had this happened?

CHAPTER FOUR

Iris still felt weak and muddled from the amount of spell energy she'd used up in order to escape from Big Nuts's house of sex. She petted her cat and scratched underneath his collar, the small bell jingling softly.

She leaned her head against Connor's shoulder, forcing air deep into her lungs. "Sorry." Her voice was little more than a whisper.

"For what?"

She loved how his voice rumbled in his chest. But what had he asked? Oh, yeah. Why she was sorry. "For being so useless right now."

"You got us out of there. I'm not sure without your spell we would have survived. By the way, he was there."

"Who was there?"

"The vampire intent on killing us."

She chuckled. "Oh. Him." She was so out of it.

"You okay?"

"No. But I will be. I need to recoup my strength. What did the bad guy look like?"

"Gary was right. He must have bought himself a spell because it was hard to see him. But he was tall, lean, light-colored eyes, dark hair. I couldn't discern his features, though."

She sighed. "Not much to go on."

"No, it isn't."

The energy of her garden flowed over her and had begun to restore her. Being in Connor's arms helped as well.

"What can I do to help you feel better?"

"Kiss me." Wait. Why had she said that?

"You want me to kiss you?" A soft chuckle left his throat.

"No, I mean yes. I mean, God, no." But it would be really nice.

Again, that man-hungry feeling returned. He'd kissed her earlier in the garden, but she'd been so overwhelmed, she hadn't been able to respond, at least for a few seconds. He'd looked distressed when he'd pulled back, searching her eyes with that heavy frown between his brows. She'd finally given in to her desire for him, in part to make sure he knew how much she wanted him, desired him.

"Connor?"

"Yes."

"I loved the kiss you gave me before. It was one of the best experiences of my life. Can we do it again?"

"Absolutely."

"I've thought about it. I think now would be good."

He smiled tenderly. "How about when you recover a little more."

After a moment, she shifted in his arms so she could look at him. Pips jumped off her lap at the same time. "You have beautiful blue eyes. I think they're one of your best features." Her gaze dropped to his lips.

"How weak are you right now?" His voice had dropped into a lower timbre, a sound that teased her between her legs.

She sat up enough to slide an arm around his neck. "My garden is helping. And being with you as well, though I'm not sure why. You seem to have an effect on me and I'm coming back fast."

She kissed him, her tongue rimming the soft fullness of his lips. She could feel her garden swaying around her, creating a breeze that carried an elixir of beautiful scents. Some were healing, others erotic. What she'd spent so much time nurturing, began to give back to her, renewing her energy with every breath, even as she kissed Connor.

The sissoo swayed above her as well.

When she drew back, Connor smoothed his fingers over her cheek. "You're so beautiful, Iris."

She felt him, felt his words and what lay beneath. She knew he'd been married before the *alter*, just as she had. But he hadn't engaged in a serious relationship since. They were a lot alike.

Violet's earlier words came back to her. *Save Connor.*

What had she meant by it?

"Connor," she began, though no other words followed. She was still a little muddled, but getting stronger by the second.

"I'm here." He searched her eyes, then leaned in and kissed her again, a brief touch of his lips to hers. "You feel like a dream to me, like you don't really exist."

At that, she smiled. "I know what you mean. I never thought I'd feel this way again."

He drifted a series of sensual kisses over her lips, one after the other. "What way?"

What had he asked? Oh, yes, the way she was feeling. She drew back enough to meet his gaze. "As though I could be in bed with you and stay there for a long time. Days maybe."

"Is that how you feel?" He looked so serious.

She nodded.

"Iris." His voice was low, hushed. "I think I'm falling for you."

Her mind slipped back to earlier in the evening and seeing the red half-hearts on Jason and Sadie's hands.

They'd been lovers.

A decade of loneliness swelled over her, putting an ache in her heart. "Me, too, but maybe we should stop."

Connor's gaze once more fell to her lips. "You're right, we should."

"Uh-huh."

When she tilted her face, inviting him, he settled his lips on hers, but more forcefully this time. She moaned, her entire body lighting up. When she parted her lips, his tongue entered her, and he took his time searching the recesses of her mouth. Then he began to plunge, a beautiful prologue. She savored each thrust that quickly became a dedicated, very familiar rhythm.

When she pulled back, she was breathing hard. "Make love to me,

Connor, right here in the garden. And right now. No more questions, or doubts, or anything. Just sex, because I think we both need this."

~~ * ~~

Connor plundered Iris's mouth, knowing he shouldn't, but unable to help himself. He'd craved her for months. Now she was in his arms and telling him she was falling for him, too.

She tasted sweet, like a ripe plum. He licked her tongue and heard her moan in response. He slid his hand over her breast, her nipple already peaked as he began to fondle her. A streak of desire shot through his cock. He glided his hand to her waist and pulled her t-shirt from her jeans, then smoothed his fingers over her stomach and up to her bra. He caressed her again through the soft fabric then plucked at her nipples.

She groaned and pushed at him, though he wasn't sure why. When he drew back, he saw that her cheeks were flushed. He was about to call a halt to everything, thinking maybe she was too weak to continue. But she suddenly leaned back just enough to take her shirt off and set her hair free from her ponytail. He held her loosely in his arms the whole time to keep her from falling backward.

She wanted this as much as he did.

His gaze was caught by the white mounds of her breasts. His jaw trembled with need. Using his arm to support her, she was able to reach behind and unclasp her bra.

His intake of breath was a slow hiss as his gaze floated over her bare breasts. Her nipples were erect and with a grunt he fell on her chest, taking as much of her left breast in his mouth as he could.

But his pants had become a serious hindrance. "Time to get rid of some of these clothes." His voice sounded hoarse to his own ears.

She eagerly slid off his lap to sit on the grass. "Shirt off," she commanded. "I want to look at you."

He smiled, knowing the effect his muscled body had on women. He was on his knees as he lost the tank.

But she held out a hand, stopping him from moving. He didn't know why, until her gaze took in his shoulders, his chest, his stomach. She shifted to her knees as well and with her hands caressed his chest, feeling him up.

The *altered* life had given him strength. He pumped iron, but only required a quarter of the time his human counterparts would need to get the defined look the Border Patrol men carried. She fondled his pecs, and he wasn't surprised when she leaned into him and took some of his flesh in her mouth.

The suckling had his cock standing straight up and begging for the same kind of attention. While she worked his chest, he unbuttoned his leathers and began pulling them down, freeing his erection.

As she continued to touch him and suck on his pecs, she kept making small moans and coos, all sorts of sounds that helped him know how much she was into him.

Was this really happening?

He'd had many fantasies about making love to her, but none of them equaled the simple touch of her tongue, her lips, her hands. A soft witch energy flowed from her as well, as much an erotic sensation as everything else she was doing.

When she leaned back, panting, he went to work on her jeans. Of course by the time he had them peeled down to her knees, he realized he had to get rid of her shoes.

He untied them as quickly as he could. But once he had the rest of her clothes off, she surrounded his cock with both hands, fondling him. He was still on his knees and his leathers had him trapped. She scooted closer, smiling up at him.

All he could do was stare at her awestruck.

"I think I know what you're feeling," she said. "It's as though we're the first people in the entire world to have ever done this."

"Your touch is like that for me."

"And how about this."

When she bent down and her warm, wet mouth surrounded the head of his cock, he groaned heavily. His breathing grew rough right away and his hips arched, thrusting his cock deeper into her mouth. She sucked at the same time, and when he pulled back, she caught the rim of his cock with her lips, then flicked her tongue quickly over the tip.

He put a hand on her shoulder and withdrew. "I'll come too soon."

She released him then rose and with both hands pushed him onto his back. He wasn't sure she'd understood his dilemma until he realized her intent was to get him naked. She made quick work of his boots and leathers.

As he lay against the cool lawn, with Iris kissing her way up his legs, he felt as though he'd dropped into heaven. He wanted to stay here forever.

He thought back to the couple on Sentinel, their half-hearts and the certainty they'd been lovers. He'd been appalled at the time, despite the fact he'd been lusting after Iris for months.

But now that he was here, in Iris's garden only a few hours later, he understood. In thirty years, he'd had a lot of very brief relationships with vampire females, some of them good, worthy women. But none of them had made him feel that maybe life would be okay. And that's what Iris did for him.

She crawled up his body, careful when she was between his legs, then kissed his abdomen and tongued his six-pack. He caressed her face at the same time, sliding his hand behind her neck. "I love what you're doing to me."

"You have a magnificent body and I intend to show a lot of appreciation."

He smiled, savoring that she was sucking his pecs again and moaning at the same time. She was as eager as he was.

When his hips arched, she rose up and straddled him. He nodded his encouragement as she reached between her legs to hold his cock in place then lowered her sex onto him.

The moment he felt her wetness, he groaned heavily once more. He was where he'd wanted to be for a long time now.

Her whole body undulated as he began to push inside her. "Oh, Connor."

Her voice sounded loud in the garden. "Do we need to worry about the neighbors?"

She shook her head. "The spell blocks the noise."

He groaned when she rolled her hips. "Thank God for your witchness."

After she'd rocked over him several times, he had an idea of his own. "Let me."

With her lips parted, she nodded then leaned over him, balancing herself with her palms planted on his chest. He began to thrust, rocking his hips and driving deeper into her each time until he was fully seated.

She cried out. "You have no idea how good this feels."

He had to disagree. "Trust me, I have an inkling."

He realized then she had tears in her eyes. "I didn't think it was possible to feel this way as a witch. I thought part of what I'd lost because of the *alter* was the ability to be passionate. But Connor, I'm coming apart here."

He grabbed her shoulders and pulled her close so that her head was on his shoulder. "It's okay. I know I said this to you earlier, but I'll say it again now: let it go."

He felt her sob again. He was buried deep, and the woman was crying. Maybe it was a witch thing, that she was communicating with him in ways not human at all, but he felt her pain and how deep it was. He closed his eyes and while she wept, he remained very still except for his hands which he used to rub her back and shoulders.

After a minute or two, her tears subsided and she grabbed for her t-shirt and wiped her nose and face. "You're such a kind man, Connor. Thank you. I don't know why that happened."

He pushed her hair away from her face. "It doesn't matter. You've been through a lot and not just tonight."

She kissed him, her body pulling on what was still hard. She moaned again, then lifted up. "I want to be on my back."

Connor's turn to moan. He caught her bottom in one hand, holding her tight against him. With great care, he rolled them both over so he could stay connected. It was a bit tricky, but he had enough girth to get the job done.

At the same time, his fangs began to emerge, something he couldn't help, something he wanted to do with Iris badly.

But now that she was beneath him, what was very male in him took over. He moved into her, all the way.

Then he went to work.

~~ * ~~

Iris rolled her head back and forth on the cool grass, her body eased with each drive of Connor's cock, each thrust like heaven.

She wasn't sure why she'd lost it, except that her grief about living in Five Bridges and being separated from all that she'd once loved and cherished, whether through death or the *alter*, had somehow come down to this moment with Connor. Now she was looking up at him, his shoulder-length hair moving in waves as he thrust, his blue eyes almost intense as he pushed into her.

She rubbed her thumb over his lips. He'd been nothing but kind throughout the entire difficult night, and now he was making love to her.

He leaned down as he thrust, connecting his chest to hers and kissing her.

She surrounded his back with her arms, gliding her hands gently over his thick muscles. She loved how he felt, moving as he was. His whole body was engaged in the rhythmic, undulations that had her breaths coming in light pants. In response, her sex pulled on him, needing him, wanting what he could give her.

She gripped his ass, loving the flex and release of his buttocks. Her sex tightened. Was this really happening?

He began slowly nudging her chin aside, farther and farther until he was licking a line up and down her neck.

She gasped, remembering. Vampire.

Her sex released a series of pulses. She was on the verge.

"May I feed, Iris? Do you trust me enough to let me feed from you?"

Once he began, he had the power to keep going until she was drained dry in what was known as a vampire thrall. It was the balance of Five Bridges. She could kill him with a touch. He could take her life once he sunk his fangs.

Her breaths came out in harsh gasps. "I didn't think I'd ever say this, Connor, but I want you to bite me more than anything else on earth right now. And yes, I trust you."

He groaned yet again and with the practice of decades, struck her throat, nipping through to the vein. When he began to suck, she cried out because she'd never imagined it would feel so incredible.

His hips were back in motion as well so she had two sensations pummeling her at once. Her body felt lit with fire as he sucked. And she was feeding Connor, taking care of his vampire blood needs.

She knew this was considered a thrall, but for some reason she was still able to move. Every account she'd heard spoke of a paralytic condition; the vampire could drink as long as he wanted. But right now she didn't care that the rules didn't completely apply to her.

She moaned, her hips rising up to push against his as he thrust. She gripped his shoulders and cried out. It all felt so good.

Suddenly, he released her neck, swiping the wounds to seal them. "Your witch blood. Iris, it's like a drug. I feel strange but really strong." His thrusts were steady and purposeful.

She caught his face with both hands. Had her blood done something to him? "Are you all right?" He looked wild, his eyes rolling in his head.

His hips began to move faster. "I'm fine. I'm better than fine. My God. Iris!"

When he focused on her once more, his eyes had a powerful glint and waves of vampire energy flowed over her, adding yet another layer of sensation. She felt his energy merge with hers, a beautiful aligning she hadn't expected.

She was one with him, in every way possible.

He held her gaze and she let herself fall into his eyes. She moved with him, moaning. Pleasure began to rise as she'd never known before. Her heart pounded in her chest.

She dug her nails into his arms as ecstasy roared toward her. It came like a locomotive, racing along, then sweeping her off the rails and high into the air.

Still holding his gaze, she screamed as searing pleasure drove through her well, up and up, capturing her heart and finally exploding through her mind.

Connor lifted up, and roared into the night. She gripped his arms, her body writhing beneath his. Just when she thought it was over, another wave swept through her and she screamed again.

Connor stayed with her, keeping the pleasure flowing. He rocked his hips while he kissed her throat, her cheeks, her lips until at last the orgasm began to subside.

She was breathing hard, Connor as well.

He rested his forearms on either side of her, supporting his muscled weight. She slid her fingers into his hair, damp from exertion. He smelled like the leather he wore, and there was just a hint of gunpowder from the shot he'd fired in Gary's office.

She loved it all, loved that the events of the night had brought them together, when nothing else could have.

He smiled faintly, and she swore he wanted to say something, but couldn't. Then a sad light entered his eyes as he leaned down to kiss her cheek, her chin and put a brief pressure on her lips.

She thought she understood. "Even if we never do this again, Connor, it was wonderful. Magical." She chuckled softly. "Unbelievable."

"It was. But it feels damn temporary."

"I know." She searched his eyes. "Will you stay here tonight? I mean through the day? Sleep in my bed? I'd love it if you would."

"I want nothing else. Besides," he glanced up at the spell over her house, "I think we'd both be safer here."

"I think you're right."

He glanced around and reached to the left where his clothes lay. He grabbed his tank and as he pulled out of her, he tucked the shirt between her legs.

She knew then what kind of husband he'd been and her heart broke all over again, for both of them and what they'd each lost because of the *alter*. He was a good man, despite that he was a vampire.

~~ * ~~

Connor shifted to recline beside Iris. Dawn wasn't pressing on him yet, though it would soon. But right now, he didn't want to leave the garden, or the moment.

He felt profoundly connected to Iris right now. He knew she'd been forced to leave a husband behind when she'd gone through her witch *alter*. Then her sister had died some time during the first year the two women had come to live in Elegance. Even so, her sadness felt deeper still, though he didn't know in what way.

His own pain was very different. Yes, he'd buried a wife, but that had been before he'd come to live in Five Bridges.

His remorse and suffering had occurred after his vampire *alter* and during his work with the Crescent Border Patrol. In the line of duty in one instance and after being abducted and shot up with blood flame in another, he'd ended up hurting and killing a lot of innocent women. Their deaths lived inside him like a wound that could never heal. He wasn't worthy of a real relationship with Iris or any woman. His time with Iris was a stolen season.

In the last thirty years, since he'd lived in Five Bridges, he'd never experienced anything as profound as what he'd just done with Iris. He had no words. He flexed his right arm. He honestly felt pumped up from her blood.

Christ, the woman's blood. Witch blood. Full of power. He'd felt the moment as well when he could have kept going and taken her life. Witches might be able to touch vampires and kill them. But once a vampire started to drink, his victim couldn't stop the process. The vampire had complete control.

That she'd been able to move at all was one more indication of her power as a witch.

His mind spiraled down into the past, to the horrendous witch massacre he'd been part of. Though his memory was spotty because of the level of blood flame he'd been given, he knew the witches had all been tied up so they couldn't employ their killing power. Reports later indicated most of the women had been drained to death.

He shuddered.

Iris put a hand on his chest. "What's wrong?"

"The past."

"Don't think about it too much, not right now. Plenty of time tomorrow."

She was right. He had Iris beside her. What else did he need?

He slid his arm beneath her shoulders and she rolled to stretch out alongside him, her arm draped over his stomach. He looked up into the tree. The cat had climbed up as well and sat beside the owl. Each peered down at them.

He chuckled, then without warning his throat grew tight and his eyes started to burn. "This is a stolen season, isn't it?"

"It is."

She lifted her face to him and offered a soft smile. He kissed her again, running his hand along the dip of her waist and the curve of her hip. The word 'love' rose to his lips. He almost used it, wanting to badly. But it was too soon and most likely, he would never have the chance. There were truths to be spoken and when they were, his time with Iris would end.

His chest felt crushed. He wanted to say something to her, to express his gratitude, but couldn't. He was feeling too much

Then she spoke several magical words all strung together. "Are you hungry? I mean I know I just fed you, but neither of us has eaten since this whole thing began. I could do sandwiches. I have a nice pumpernickel bread and pastrami. No fancy mustard, though. Oh, and a really strong Stout beer."

He groaned. "You have no idea how perfect that sounds. I mean it."

She rose to her feet. She drew the tank from between her legs, but kept hold of it as she gathered up her own clothes and her gun and holster.

Gaining his feet, he did the same with his belongings then followed after her as she headed to the back door. Along the way, he glanced into her bedroom, really liking that it overlooked the garden as well from a pair of French doors. Glancing up, the spell looked as strong as ever. From his point of view, this would be a solid place to remain through the day.

Once inside, she turned to look at him over her bare shoulder. "I'm going to clean up a little then I'll be right back."

"Anything I can do?" he asked. He set his clothes on the couch.

"You're fine. I'll only be a couple of minutes. It'll be quicker if I fix the meal myself."

"Okay, but let me know if you need anything."

He put his tank and leathers back on, grateful he had a clean change of clothes for tomorrow. And he'd definitely want to shower before bed.

When Iris returned, he watched a whirlwind whip around the kitchen as she moved from cupboard to fridge to sink and back. Within a couple of minutes, he was chowing down on an excellent sandwich.

An hour later and ready for a good day's sleep, Iris stared down at the faded pink-and-green flowered quilt on her bed. She hadn't slept beside a man in ten years. Though the queen-size mattress had been more than enough for her, it seemed to shrink but in a good way. Connor was a big man.

While he showered, she drew the covers back, turned the sheet down and plumped the pillows. She felt oddly nervous, knowing she'd be sleeping beside him. In many ways, she barely knew him.

Her room was simple, with an antique chest of drawers, a full-length mirror, a basket of dried flowers on the floor, smallish oak end tables. The French doors served as the main window. More light came from a long, narrow, diamond-paned panel of glass above the bed but only a foot from the ceiling.

Because of the protective spell, she'd felt comfortable leaving the French doors wide. She loved fresh air in a bedroom and early March had perfect temperatures in the desert to make it possible.

Slipping off her robe, she climbed into bed. She rarely slept in a nightgown and saw no need to wear one now. Besides, she was pretty sure Connor wouldn't mind at all.

She pulled the sheet up high enough to cover her breasts, then turned on her side. She set her gaze on her garden, enjoying the beauty she could see easily at night because of her *alter* vision.

As the shower drummed, what she didn't understand was what she was supposed to do with Connor. Part of her wanted to keep him tied up in her bedroom for a really long time. Another part thought she would be wise to cut her losses and run.

All this flurry of sexual craving and now satisfaction still didn't mean she could have a real relationship with him. She'd felt him during the first few minutes of being with him on Sentinel Bridge. He had a darkness in his soul, and she had no idea why. Something had happened in his past, an event that had turned him inside out and probably something beyond the way he'd been ushered into an *altered* state.

Her concerns, however, wouldn't be eased in one night. Fatigue from all she'd been through began having an effect. She breathed deeply and sleep curled through her mind.

The night had been unbelievable on every possible front, but her stomach was full, she'd had extraordinary sex with the man of her dreams, and now she needed rest. She closed her eyes and began drifting off.

She woke up just enough to feel Connor slide into bed beside her. Without thinking and maybe because she was half asleep, she scooted close to him. He was on his back and when he lifted his arm, she planted herself firmly against his side, as she had earlier on the grass. She rested an arm on his abdomen and angled a knee over his muscular thighs.

The heat of his body had an effect and she disappeared into her dreams.

When she woke up, the afternoon desert light was on the wane, the early March air cool. Connor was lying on his side and still asleep when she slid from bed.

She pulled a flowered dress from her closet, something she preferred to wear when she rose and well before she got ready for TPS duty. She enjoyed her down time first thing at night. Collecting the rest of her things, she shut the door quietly behind her.

She used the bathroom to get dressed, to apply a little mascara then a brow pencil to make her arched eyebrows behave. A touch of lip gloss and she was ready to go.

When she reentered the hall, she didn't head to the living area but to the second bedroom in her house, the one that served as her library. She opened the door and went first to the white basinet in the corner draped with a lavender and green handmade quilt that her mother had made just for Anna. A long skirt of gathered white eyelet and lace covered the entire body and base of the basinet.

For a moment, she was drawn back to the events that had brought her to Five Bridges. She'd been at a college graduation party for one of Violet's friends since she knew the family well. They had a private home in north Scottsdale not far from a local high-end resort, but a long distance away from Five Bridges. Her husband had been out of town on business. She'd felt perfectly safe.

But afterward, while walking down the hill to her car, they'd been abducted by several Elegance warlocks and shot up with flame drugs each bearing the additional witch *alter* serum.

By the time she woke up in the trunk of an unknown car, she no longer felt like herself. Her body had already started the irreversible process. Six months pregnant, she started cramping badly. She was also deep inside Five Bridges; she'd been trafficked.

Labor had begun almost immediately and she'd held her stomach in agony, her heart shattering at the same time. Babies never survived the *alter*. Fetuses could often tolerate harsh levels of the various flame drugs, but not the *alter* serum itself.

She'd called Violet's name, but she'd been alone, her head angled painfully on top of a smelly spare tire. She'd had no idea where her younger sister had been taken.

When she began to bleed heavily, her abductors had abandoned her, tossing her onto the side of the road to die. Eliza, her wonderful witch mentor, had found her and taken her to an Elegance hospital. In that sense, she'd been fortunate.

Violet's fate had been horrendous. From the time she'd been abducted, she'd been strung out on blood flame and used as a prostitute. For six weeks, Eliza had hunted for her and finally bought her from the low-life warlocks who'd been handling her.

Elegance Territory, like Crescent, had a dark soulless side. Iris had begun working for the Tribunal because it was the only public entity that had as its mission statement a goal to improve life in Five Bridges. She hoped one day she'd become a force for good, but she didn't see much changing any time soon. There was simply too much evil in their world to have high expectations.

Once she'd buried her baby, Eliza had helped her come to terms with her *altered* state and the loss of her little girl, whom she'd named Anna. Eliza had recommended bringing some of her things from her normal life into Five Bridges. The basinet and baby quilt had been two of the things. Her bedroom furniture had been in her Phoenix home as well.

Saying good-bye to her husband had been the hardest thing she'd ever done. But she'd had no choice but to let him go. It was the only thing she could do given how changed she was. None of the five species were allowed to live anywhere but in the designated territories. And she wouldn't have asked him to reside in Five Bridges for all the money in the world. He hadn't put up much of a fight, but they'd both wept as much for the loss of their child as for their marriage.

Her parents had been overjoyed to learn she was alive and to see her again, yet devastated by the cruel turn of events. When she'd begun work as a TPS officer, she'd been given a passport and had been able to visit them a few times during the first year until Violet's death. After that, she called once a year to give a report. But she'd let them go as well. It hurt them too much to know she was separated from them forever because she'd gone through the *alter*.

Her two brothers had grown up and married. Grandchildren were the order of the day. For her own sake, she needed her parents to forget the one remaining witch daughter who was living out her life in a constant horror show in Five Bridges. Iris could never go back to her former life and she'd never allow her family to visit her in her world.

She'd learned to embrace her witch life, however, and live it to the fullest. Part of that included grieving for Anna, even though she'd died ten years ago.

By long habit, Iris let her grief flow and to her surprise it didn't feel quite as pressing as usual. She turned toward the doorway. Was it because of Connor?

She thought it might be. Despite the difficulties of the night before and no doubt more challenges tonight, his presence had reminded her of the good things life had to offer.

Turning away from the basinet, she could have sat down, paid some bills, checked her emails, but what she really wanted was a strong cup of coffee.

~~ * ~~

Connor sat on the end of Iris's bed, staring at his fresh clothes in neat piles on the dresser to his left. He'd already shaved and showered and had come back to the bedroom to find his clothes laid out as well as his weapons. She'd also left a gun cleaning kit for him, which had made him smile. She owned a gun, so she knew. Before showering, he'd taken care of his Glock having fired it at Gary's and several times earlier in the week.

He recalled when Iris had suggested he bring a couple of changes of clothes over and how right she'd been.

He'd thought the day's sleep would have eased his head. Instead, he felt burdened all over again, maybe with guilt. Hell, probably.

He huffed another heavy sigh, probably for the tenth time. He put on clean, black leathers and his boots, another tank as well. He slid his reinforced belt through the loops and buckled. He checked his gun; it was good to go. But he wouldn't clip it on until they were ready to head out.

Same with his short-sword, which was safe in its sheath. He hadn't used it during his time with Iris so far. He hoped to hell he didn't have to. Bullets were one thing. But when the fighting turned to blades, blood flowed. He was glad she wasn't squeamish, but he hoped she didn't have to prove herself tonight.

As he moved into the living area, he caught sight of Iris out in her garden and his frown deepened. She was sipping coffee and looked really perplexed. She then leaned over a spray of some kind of red flower and stroked the petals. Was it his imagination or did the flower bob as though there was a breeze when all the other plants remained static. Right. She was talking to her plants again and apparently they were answering.

She wore a flowery dress, snug at her narrow waist and flaring over her hips. A slight wind moved through the garden and lifted the hem of her dress, revealing long slender legs.

She wasn't wearing a ponytail. Instead her dark brown hair hung almost to her waist. It was straight and gleamed in the twilight. All the species of Five Bridges preferred the night, a result of the *alter* drugs. Some could tolerate the early gray of dawn or twilight as Iris was now. Not vampires.

He pounded a fist against his chest a couple of times, trying to steel himself against his growing love for Iris. Once she knew the truth about him, she'd despise him. Which meant soon he'd have to tell her what he'd done, that he'd been involved in a witch massacre nine years ago. But he dreaded seeing the look on her face once she found out.

She'd never be able to be with him then, which was another layer of guilt. He should have confessed the truth last night, but all he'd wanted was to make love with her at least once.

Confession would end their stolen season as quickly as it had begun. He'd hinted about it, but he'd been unable to be specific. Even the thought of saying the words aloud, that he'd raped and killed women of her kind, twisted his gut into a knot.

His *altered* state had stripped him down to his bones. He had nothing to give Iris or any woman for that matter. He lived a loner's existence, a night-hunting creature who had to get his blood-needs met on a regular basis, and who battled the drug infestation of their Five Bridges world. This was his life. And it wasn't fit to be shared with a woman.

He debated telling her the truth right now because the more time he spent with her, the more he longed to have a life with her.

His decision arrived. He had to tell her. She would despise him, but it couldn't be helped. Worse, she'd have to accept his continued presence in her life right now because he wasn't about to leave her, not when some madman wanted her dead. His goal was simple, to do everything in his power to keep her safe.

He left the open French doors, moved into the kitchen and poured himself a cup of coffee. He prepared his speech.

But as he returned to the dining area, she'd started back to the house, walking along the green patch of grass. She waved and a smile lit up her face. She was glad to see him.

His breath got stuck somewhere between his lungs and his throat. "Oh, shit." There it was again, desire raging through his body and attacking his heart. And worse, he loved her. He couldn't deny it any longer.

He loved the witch, Iris Meldeere.

And he didn't think he could tell her the truth, not now. Maybe, when they figured out who was hunting them and brought the man to justice. Yeah, maybe then.

"Good evening," she said, moving across the threshold. "Sleep well?"

He nodded, but he knew he was scowling. He could feel his face pinched up. "Fine, thanks." He took a sip of his coffee.

"What's wrong?"

"Nothing much. Just worried about tonight." Yeah, nothing much.

She shrugged, tilting her head. "Me, too. First, though, scrambled eggs and toast?"

His resolve shrank to nothing in the face of her simple suggestion. She'd ended their lovemaking with an offer of food and had begun the next night in the same way. He wasn't sure a man needed much more than sex, food, and a woman he loved. "Eggs and toast would be great."

She moved into the kitchen and washed her hands. The whirlwind returned. She hauled eggs, butter and bread out of the fridge, shutting the door with her foot as she moved swiftly away. When she started cracking eggs into a bowl, she called over her shoulder. "Turn the news on, would you? I want to know what's being said about the bombing of Sentinel."

"Will do."

He found the remote next to the small flat screen that she kept across from the dining table.

He pressed the power button and, no surprise, a commercial came up first.

"Just mute it."

He pressed the mute button and settled the remote on the table. He sat down, but had nothing to say, his guilt still dragging him down. The time to speak had passed and he let it go. For now.

He sipped his coffee instead, with one eye on the TV. When the news anchor returned, he watched for pictures of the bridge, but the focus appeared to be on a sex scandal involving an elementary school teacher who operated a porn site at night.

Iris remained busy in the kitchen. She occasionally glanced at the TV, but didn't appear to want to make conversation. Maybe her thoughts were drawn inward as well.

~~ * ~~

Iris buttered the toast, then swirled the eggs in the hot pan now and then. She'd made triple her usual portion; Connor was a big man.

She'd awakened with something on her mind, but she didn't know exactly how to frame it. Her thoughts from the time she'd risen from bed had been focused on one particular part of the lovemaking last night, when Connor had fed from her. It had been extremely erotic, one of the best sexual moments of her life. But that wasn't what snagged her thoughts.

She tried to recall Connor's exact words right after feeding. He'd said something about feeling 'better than all right'. And he'd seemed so much more powerful. Even physically his muscles had looked pumped. She could only suppose it wasn't normal for him since he'd seemed surprised by it.

When the eggs were done, she slid them onto a pair of stoneware plates then added the toast. She put a fork on each plate and had just started over to the table when it hit her, what was really on her mind. "Your energy, Connor. It merged with mine."

She moved into the dining area and Connor, his mug to his lips, returned the cup to the table. "What? What are you talking about?"

She set the plates down, sliding one toward him. Glancing at the TV, she decided to shut it off completely. Apparently, the sex scandal was the only thing the news was going to focus on.

She sat down and forced herself to eat a few bites.

"You realize you're holding me in suspense."

She aimed her fork at his eggs. "Eat. Then I'll tell you."

"They smell wonderful, so I won't argue with you."

She glanced at him and saw the twisted smile on his lips. She felt it all over again, the raw attraction she felt for him. Suddenly, she was out of her seat, leaning toward him before she knew what she was doing. She caught his face in her hands and planted a kiss on his lips.

When she drew back, his brows rose. "What was that for?"

She shook her head as she resumed her seat. "Just wanted to."

She focused on her meal once more, forcing herself to slow down because she kept wolfing her meal.

Connor finally reached over and grabbed her hand. "I need you to calm down. Your witch energy is riding my skin like a dirt bike going downhill."

She lifted her brows and laughed. "That bad, huh?"

"Yes. I don't know what it is, but I seem to be very sensitive to you."

She settled her fork on her plate. "And that's what I wanted to talk to you about. You're not going to like this, Connor, but I think I need to enthrall you."

CHAPTER FIVE

Iris doubted Connor would go for it. After all, any citizen of Five Bridges brought under a witch's thrall was completely vulnerable. And that included powerful vampires, who served as Border Patrol officers for Crescent Territory.

Connor set his own fork down, then leaned back in his chair. He'd made good work of his scrambled eggs and toast. "Okay, why? And what's this about our energies merging?"

At least he hadn't refused her outright. "Because we have an unusual connection and we need to explore it. I think it means something, but I'm not sure what. Do you recall how you felt right after you fed from me? Can you describe it?"

He shook his head, his gaze scattering for a moment. She let him process.

Even as she waited, Iris knew instinctively she'd wandered into dangerous territory, and that wasn't the witch in her talking, but her female intuition.

Setting aside Connor's male gorgeousness and that he'd given her the best sex of her life the night before, she knew something was off with him and not because he was a vampire. He'd suffered in some way that had shattered him deep inside, maybe when he first went through the *alter*.

He was a broken, damaged man and all the spells in the world couldn't fix that. Only Connor could reach into his own soul and perform the healing he needed. But like most men, she doubted he had a clue where to start, even if he wanted to.

Despite all that, the vampire had a pull on her she'd never experienced in her life. He was tall, strong and rugged looking. Some vampires, like those addicted to any of the numerous flame drugs, eventually started looking like their movie brethren with extremely pale skin and almost skeletal bodies. They were hard to look at, especially if they flashed some fang.

But Connor was a different animal, and her heart beat hard as she waited for his answer.

As for her enthrallment powers, these were mostly a matter of long-term training by her witch elder, a good-hearted woman named Eliza who lived a very secluded life at the cul-de-sac end of Iris's street. She had a full acre to her name and Iris had gotten many cuttings, tubers, and full grown plants from the woman when she'd begun creating her own spell-support garden.

Eliza had trained her to focus inward on her heart, the source of desire, then to *want* to bring the object of her thrall under her control. For whatever reason, Iris had found the process simple and exhilarating. The latter reaction, however, had warned her to be very careful when and how she employed this ability. The spell at Big Nuts's place was a perfect example.

Although on some level, she still couldn't believe she'd been able not only to enthrall everyone in two rooms, but to release part of the thrall selectively. Connor had been exempted and when needed, Big Nuts as well.

Connor rose from his seat. "I've narrowed it down to this. Your blood gave me power, real physical power. I could have fought better right then if we'd been attacked. It was an amazing sensation. And ever since, I've felt connected to you in a way I don't get. I've also craved repeating the whole thing. If you feel a need to enthrall me, I'll allow it."

Iris had reached a serious crossroads in her life. If she moved forward and attempted the thrall, she had a powerful prescience she'd never be able to go back, that her life would be forever changed.

The problem was she didn't know in what way, and that scared her.

Yet something had happened during the lovemaking to her as well, beyond the pleasure and fulfillment of the act. She thought back to the moment their energies had become one. She glanced up at Connor who stood nearby, arms over his chest. He frowned at her, watching her closely as though he too understood the importance of this moment.

"You don't have to do this, Iris. If you have any doubt, it might be better to wait, to hold back. But I'm open."

She rose from her chair and moved close to him, placing her hand on his arm. "Do you feel that?"

"I do. Like a soft jolt of electricity, not as bad as before."

She offered a half-smile. "No dirt bikes racing downhill?"

"No. This is good. Pleasant even. But tell me what you're looking for, what you hope to achieve."

"That's just it. I don't know. I'm going with my instincts. There's something unusual between us and it might be critical. I don't pretend to understand how you and I came to be together. But Violet actually guards your presence here, my garden seems to adore you if you haven't yet noticed, and both Sebastien and Pips have bestowed their not-easily-won approval.

"All these elements have my witch senses lit up. Beyond that, I don't have an answer for you. But would you be willing to explore it with me? And for that, I have to ask the hard question: Do you trust me?"

For some reason, as Connor stared back at her and appeared to consider his answer, she felt as though her entire future depended on him saying yes to her. Again, she didn't know why. But her witchness was in full bore.

"You could have spelled me to get me to acquiesce."

"Yes, but why would I do that?"

Connor's stern expression relaxed. "The fact that you responded with exactly that question is the reason I'm saying yes."

Iris blinked several times. She honestly didn't understand and felt as though she'd missed something. "Connor, I've never used my powers to trick anyone. And you have no idea how easy it would be to employ my spells all the time, even to get a better position in line for coffee. But I don't do that."

"The more I'm around you," he gestured to the protection spell covering her property, "the more I'm understanding your level of power. So, how do we do this, witch?"

"I'll need to be close because you're as strong as you are. And I'll want to touch you."

His lips twisted. "I'm liking this already."

Her heart gave a sudden powerful jump, and she had to take a moment to breathe. She knew then what the real problem was for her: She liked Connor in an essential way, the kind of man he was and how he treated her.

"Me, too," she responded quietly.

She then pulled herself together, and began focusing her witch energy on the process of thrall. She settled herself within a few inches of his entire body until she felt his aura connecting with hers. She held her palm close to his face. "I'll have to touch you, otherwise I won't be able to do this. You're too powerful. Is that okay? Just to be clear, right now you have control and you might not have any once I begin the process."

He smiled. "Go for it."

"Okay." As she shifted her hand to place three of her fingers alongside his cheek, though well away from his vulnerable temple, she tapped into her ability to enthrall. She focused on her desire to bring Connor under her power.

A warm stream of energy began to flow from her heart, through her veins, to finally warm her right arm then her hand where she connected with his cheek.

The thrall began to release into Connor's body, though not without difficulty. She'd been right. He was very powerful and she couldn't have completed the process without the physical connection. This was a different kind of enthrallment from the spell she'd cast at Gary's sex club, but almost as intense even though she was dealing with only one person.

Connor never shifted eye-contact, another indication just how much power he had as a vampire. A lesser man would have lost a certain level of consciousness by now. Instead, Connor retained full use of his mind. Yet at the same time, she knew her thrall had engaged him.

~~ * ~~

Connor had never felt like this in his entire *altered* existence. The sensation of Iris's thrall was seductive in a surprising way. He'd felt her energy begin to flow into his mind so he knew her power was having an effect. But instead of drifting into a strange drugged out state, as enthrallment had been described to him a hundred times, he felt more aware and more relaxed than he'd ever been before.

In addition, he could see Iris with great clarity and not just her beautiful, dark brown eyes or the peaches-and-cream complexion of her skin. Instead, his vision traveled deep inside her, to the parts that hurt and cried out for relief as well as the grief she lived with because of her *alter*.

Violet's death was uppermost in her mind and another loss that seemed equally as painful, though he didn't know the source. He also sensed her deep disappointment in the Tribunal and a terrible ongoing pain at the general suffering within all five territories of their world.

He saw the beauty of her soul laid out for him like a feast, as though he could devour her right now if he wanted. In an ironic twist, he knew he could hurt her badly as well, crush the essence of her and that he hadn't expected. But all he wanted to do was gather up her pain and hold it close until it melted away. If only he could do that for her?

He also saw how much she desired him, that her craving for him matched his own need and lust for her.

"Iris," he whispered.

"This wasn't what I expected."

"I know." He took her in his arms and crushed her lips with his own. He expected resistance. Instead, she embraced him with an arm around his neck and parted her lips for him, all the while keeping her fingers against his cheek.

He pierced her with his tongue and began a steady drive in and out of her mouth, letting her know what he would do to her the moment she gave permission.

He stepped into her just enough to let her feel what had grown hard and ready for her. He even arched his hips in a rhythm to match the thrusts of his tongue.

She groaned, and he pulled her tighter against him so that his whole body moved against hers. He felt her work to remain the contact of her fingers against his face to sustain the thrall.

Her breasts tightened and released in response to his embrace so that except for the presence of their clothes, he was making love to her.

It would take so little to move her to the couch and to finish what he'd started.

But just like that, she drew back, took her fingers from his face, and her thrall left his mind.

He felt odd, as though a warm blanket had been whipped away from him, leaving him cold.

He didn't release her fully, however, but held her gaze, wanting to understand everything he'd just experienced. Another part of him was also ready to take her back to bed if she said the word.

Her eyes were wide. "How did you do that?"

"Do what?"

"You saw me. You saw all of me and it wasn't right."

He shook his head. "Are you blaming me? This was your thrall, not mine. I can't help it if the process allowed me to see you." He grew very still because tears had once more bloomed in her eyes. "Iris, I didn't mean to hurt you."

When she pulled away, he let her go. He could see she was overwhelmed again and why wouldn't she be? Maybe she'd enthralled him, but something about their connection had allowed him to know the deepest part of her. If he was in her shoes, he'd be upset as well. Hell, he'd be pissed.

She began to pace, moving into the living area and out into the garden.

~~ * ~~

Of all the things that had happened between them over the past two nights, this one had upset her the most.

She was the witch. She had enthralled him. So, why had it turned out he could take a trip all the way into her soul? It should have been the other way around.

As she walked through the garden, she forced herself to calm down. She needed to think this through, to try to understand what it meant or what it could mean in terms of her abilities as a witch and Connor's vampire connection to her.

She glanced up at the protective spell and discovered that a new swirl had entered the pattern, steel gray in color and very strong, very *masculine.*

She took a moment to analyze the spell. She closed her eyes and extended her hands palms up. She felt the full length of it and there it was, Connor's signature. He was now part of the protective spell. What the hell was going on?

And when had his signature intruded?

She knew, however, exactly when it had happened, right in the middle of the lovemaking. He'd looked wild and full of power. Yes, that's when he'd infused part of his strength into the spell. She was dumbstruck all over again. How could a vampire be part of a spell like this?

"Connor? Can you come here?"

She shifted in his direction and saw that he was standing in the dining area. Having turned the TV back on, he was staring at it. He also seemed distressed.

She began moving in his direction even before he called out. "Iris, you've got to see this. Now."

When she crossed the threshold, she heard the female anchor say, "We'll have more news about the massacre in Rotten Row, after this."

Before the station cut to commercial, Iris saw the crime scene from the helicopter's camera as it panned back. There were a dozen Crescent

Border Patrol SUVs present with lights flashing, several ambulances, and black body bags lined up on the street.

She drew close to Connor. A discussion about his signature in her spell could wait. He muted the commercial.

"What happened?" she asked. "That was Big Nuts's club, right?"

He nodded. "Yep. And apparently, they're all dead. But I can't help but think it's no coincidence we were in Rotten Row the night before."

Iris frowned. "Do you really think this vampire, the one who's after us, did this?"

"My instincts are shouting at me that this is our guy. I just don't know how he could have pulled it off by himself."

"Maybe he wasn't alone."

"That's my thought, too." He pulled out his cell. "I'm going to call one of my fellow officers who works Rotten Row and get some facts."

When he made the call, he put the phone on speaker then set it on the table between them.

"Crescent Border Patrol. How may I direct your call?"

"Lily Hansen."

"One moment."

A woman's voice came on the line. "Dispatch. Lily Hansen."

"Lily, Connor here."

"Connor, thank God you're okay."

"I'm fine."

"But Sentinel … and you didn't call in." She sounded worried.

"I know, and I'm sorry about that. Got a lot going on. But right now I need to speak with Vaughn. I just heard about Rotten Row, and I may have information for him. Have him call me."

"I'll get on it right now."

When Lily ended the call, Iris asked, "Don't you have his cell number?"

"It doesn't work that way in Crescent when we're on duty. We can place outgoing calls, but all other communication goes directly through Lily and her gang. We tried it the other way, but the numbers got out and our phones got jammed up quick."

"Understood. And who's Vaughn?"

"A good friend. He's worked Border Patrol almost as long as I have. He's also been assigned to Rotten Row for the past two years."

Iris didn't know Officer Vaughn, but if he was a good friend, she knew Connor trusted him.

When the commercials ended, Connor unmuted the TV. The female anchor shared the gruesome stats. "More than forty dead so far, but the count isn't final. The owner of the club, Gary Smith, was not found among the bodies. Wait a minute. I have Jose on location with a live feed from the canal near Amado Bridge in Crescent Territory. Go ahead Jose."

Amado again.

The Hispanic reporter was standing with a finger up to his earpiece. Behind him a body lay on the ground covered in a white sheet. "Thanks, Evelyn. We've just had confirmation that this is the body of Gary Smith, owner of the House of Big Sex. And apparently, he's missing the part of his anatomy that gave him his famous nickname."

"Jesus," Connor murmured.

"No kidding." Iris felt a chill go straight through her. The reporter spoke for another thirty seconds but had nothing to add to the basic info. There were no suspects, no one saw anything.

Typical of Five Bridges.

~~ * ~~

Connor stared at the body on the ground behind the reporter. Big Nuts had been alive a few hours ago. Now he was dead.

He tried to picture what kind of force could have overcome Gary's powerful security entourage and his gaze slid to Iris. As a witch, she'd been able to incapacitate them. If either he or Iris had been motivated, they could have done some killing. But that's not who either of them were.

But what about the vampire he'd seen in Gary's club? If he'd used a witch's spell to disguise his identity, maybe he'd employed a dark witch's talent for a lot more than that.

His phone rang, breaking his train of thought. Vaughn's name came up on the screen. "This is him."

Iris nodded. She had her arms crossed tight over her chest, and her lips were pinched together. He could relate.

He tapped the front of the phone to answer, but kept it flat on the table, on speaker. "Vaughn. Thanks for getting back to me."

"Connor, good to hear your voice. We've got a mess out at Big Nuts's place. They're all dead."

"I've seen the footage. That's some rough stuff you've got over there. But how did they die?"

"Looks like it was a witch, using her killing power."

"A witch?" And there it was. The missing piece.

"Yeah, and a damn powerful one. She somehow got into the place and had a field day. She also employed a blade, or had someone with her who did. She even killed the sex workers as well as their clients."

Frowning, he glanced at Iris, who in turn offered a bemused shrug.

Connor glanced at the TV, which had switched from Big Nuts back to Rotten Row. "Vaughn, I'm looking at a live copter feed of Gary's place. Are you okay out there?" He knew what the local businesses could get like when their clientele got disrupted.

"We're okay for now. We've got the scene contained and enough officers to keep the locals from rioting. But I won't mind getting the hell out of here. You know this area. The owners only care about one thing and for that the traffic needs to move and keep moving. But before I answer any more of your questions, you have to tell me what happened out at Sentinel Bridge. How the hell did you survive the blast?"

Connor held out his hand to Iris. She immediately unfolded her arms and settled her hand in his. "The witch I was with, a TPS officer, had a premonition and I took her at her word. Maybe a second after I headed into the air with her, the bridge blew. It was a close call."

"When we learned you'd survived, believe me, there was celebrating down at the station. But why didn't you call in, let us know you were okay?"

Connor glanced at Iris once more.

She nodded. "Tell him everything."

"Wait. Is the witch there right now? With you?"

"Yes. We were both set-up, and we're trying to get to the bottom of it. But Gary was involved. He confessed that someone had paid him a lot of money to make sure I was sent out to Amado Bridge and later, Sentinel. The TPS officer was given the same orders, to both places."

"Both of you? That doesn't make sense."

"Believe me, we can't find the connection either."

"So, we've got a dangerous rogue witch on our hands and what else?"

"One of ours. A vampire."

There was silence for a moment, then, "You're saying a vampire and a witch are working together? That's insane."

He glanced down at his hand holding Iris's. "I know."

Iris drew a little closer and covered their joined hands with one of her own. He met her worried gaze.

Connor continued, "In my opinion, the massacre confirms it. The vampire who paid off Big Nuts was in the club. I saw him. But he was be-spelled, so I couldn't get a decent visual. Another indication he was probably working with a witch. In fact, it explains a lot." He told Vaughn the essentials of their visit to the club, then asked, "Have you seen any of the security footage? Gary had an excellent system in place, and Officer Meldeere and I are probably on it, as well as the vampire, maybe even the witch."

"It's been trashed."

Connor blew the air from his cheeks. "This guy is good."

"Yeah, but who is he and what witch has he joined forces with over in Elegance?"

Iris released his hand and moved away. Connor watched her start to pace again, a frown between her brows.

"I have no idea. But he's well-connected. Easton sent me specifically out to the first bridge as well as Sentinel and Donaldson at the Trib sent Iris, that is, Officer Meldeere to both places as well."

Vaughn snorted, but lowered his voice. "And you've just named two of the most corrupt bureaucrats Five Bridges has on its payroll. You're right. This vampire has clout of some kind, maybe the backing of one of the cartels. But listen, I've got to go. Easton is out here and he's about to go ballistic because I'm on the phone. I'm here if you need me. You know that, right?"

"I do."

"And when all this is over, we'll grab a beer. In the meantime, stay alive for fuck's sake. Crescent needs you."

Connor ended the call, a pit between his brows. "A dark witch. Jesus."

Iris moved close to him once more. "What do you think an attack on Gary and his club means, because for the life of me, I don't get it. If Big Nuts was to be believed, the same man paid Gary to set us up."

"Big Nuts wasn't exactly known for his discretion. The killer probably wanted that loose end tied up."

"Maybe. But why kill off everyone else in the club?"

Connor shrugged. "The same reason he tortured Jason and Sadie. He could have killed them outright. Instead, his sick mind needed to hurt them, which means we're looking at a sadist, probably a pair of them."

He watched a shudder pass through Iris. "You're probably right, and if any place is designed to breed the criminally insane, Five Bridges is that place."

Connor nodded. "But why you and me? We'd never even met until last night."

Iris tilted her head. "I think we need to start back at the top, at Sentinel. We know those two were romantically involved, but what else do we know about them?"

"I've already told you my connection to Jason. He was with me at that tragic shooting. And you knew Sadie at the Tribunal. But did you work on any cases with her?"

"Let me think." She closed her eyes, and he let her be. When she opened them, her eyes were narrowed. "Only one time that I can recall. Donaldson had asked me to close a file on a missing woman, and I'd been in pretty close contact with the husband, Evan Pierce. His wife, Heather, had been abducted at a Christmas Party. This was nine years ago, maybe longer. Anyway, I was able to make excellent progress, then suddenly I was shut down. Sadie was the one who delivered Donaldson's orders. But that's the only encounter I had with her."

"Was she working for Donaldson back then as his assistant?"

"You know, I think she was a temp at the time. She'd been filling in that night because Donaldson's assistant was out sick. And he's had the same one from the time I came on board."

Connor thought this through. "And what about this man, Evan, who lost his wife. Did you ever speak with him again?"

"I went to see him in Phoenix to tell him that the case had been shut down. He'd been very accepting at that point. He knew enough about Five Bridges to understand the chances of getting his wife out alive and unharmed were slim. But are you thinking he's involved somehow?"

Connor shook his head. "Just trying to piece things together."

"Well, Evan is human, not *altered*. He wouldn't be any kind of threat here in our world."

"No, he wouldn't."

Iris shook her head slowly. "I hated that case. Evan was so in love with his wife. It reminded me of all that I'd lost."

"Did you ever find out what happened to his wife?"

Her phone rang and she lifted finger. "I should take this." With the phone still on speaker, she answered the call. "Meldeere."

A woman's voice came on the line. "Iris?"

Iris's lips curved. "That's me."

"Oh, thank God, you're okay."

"Hi, Faith. I am. Thanks."

"How you holdin' up, sweetheart? We all saw the news footage that a Crescent BP officer got you off the bridge before it blew."

"He did."

"I wish you'd called in to let us know you were all right, but I'm sure you were pretty shaken up."

"Horribly. But is that why you've called? I mean if it is, that's fine and it really is wonderful to hear your voice."

"Actually," Connor heard Faith sigh. "Donaldson came down here a couple of minutes ago. He scowled the whole time. He said he didn't care that you almost died, he needed you on another assignment. Pronto."

Another set-up. Shit. Adrenaline flooded Connor's heart and veins. He moved close to Iris, sliding his arm around her waist. Now that he knew it was possible they were dealing with a pair of homicidal maniacs, Connor didn't want Iris anywhere near them.

Faith continued, "We've got an incident in Crescent that Donaldson wants you to check out. It's in the central section and pretty far from that mess down in Rotten Row. Have you been following those killings?"

"I have."

"Brutal."

"Yeah, they are. So what's the incident?"

"Right. Four or more vampires out near Tonopah Bridge. Looks like a drug deal gone bad, or something. But that's all the info I have. I don't know if they're dead, or hopped up on flame, or what. FYI, the canal over there has been breached and there's water flowing beneath the bridge on the ditch side, not sure how much though."

Iris's brown eyes were wide, and he could see her pulse beating fast in her throat. "Got it. I'll head out there in the next few minutes. Was there anything else?"

"No, but call me when you've assessed the situation."

"Donaldson's orders?"

"No. Those are mine." She lowered her voice. "I just don't want you getting killed because our prick-of-a-boss has taken some kind of pay-off. But that's all I'm going to say."

Iris smiled and Connor could feel some of the tension leave her body. "You're the best, Faith. Later."

Tonopah Bridge.

The moment she ended the call, Connor dropped down in the nearest chair. Their enemy was bringing them back full circle in a way, to one of the crimes that had wrecked him as a man. He hadn't been out to Tonopah Bridge in a long time.

Iris moved close. "What's going on?"

"That bastard is fucking with me. He knows too damn much about my life."

Iris pulled a chair close. "Is Tonopah where that pregnant woman died? The one with a gun strapped to her wrist?"

"Yes."

Connor leaned forward, clasping his hands between his knees, his forearms on his thighs. He didn't want to talk about it again. But the memory rose up like a dragon, blasting him once more. He would never forget her lovely green eyes, watching him as he approached. They'd been panicked at first, then resolution had come over her face.

Iris spoke quietly. "Tell me what happened."

He decided to launch in. "About nine, nine-and-a-half years ago, I'd been on the job awhile, but it had been a hellish night. Two of the officers I worked with had been shot and killed. We'd had so many runners out, so many gun battles, that when I took this call about a runner not far from Tonopah Bridge, I was in a bad way. One of the men we lost was a good friend.

"When I saw the runner, I was pissed. She was heading up the wash, loaded with drugs. Worse, I could see she had a gun in her hand. I yelled for her to stop or I'd shoot. She did stop and sat in the dirt waiting. She looked resigned, then she said to me, 'The baby stopped moving.'

"I saw then she was pregnant. The next thing I knew she was lifting her arm and the pistol flashed in front of me. On instinct, I fired, shot her in the chest."

"Did she get a shot off? Were you hurt?"

He shook his head. "She couldn't. It wasn't a real gun and they'd taped it to her wrist."

"Oh, God. She'd wanted to die."

He nodded. "She was so thin." He touched his neck. "She had the blood flame rash on her neck. She was emaciated, strung out, bruised all to hell. She was un-*altered*, one of the reasons she was so weak. She'd been badly used."

"And she was sure her baby had died."

"Yes."

He hadn't spoken of the incident in years. The pain came rushing back, the horror that he'd killed a woman enslaved in his world through no fault of her own.

"Did you ever find out who she was?"

He shook his head. "I did what investigating I could, but it always ended a level or two up the food chain, then got canned. I knew not to push. Besides, this woman was one of thousands I'd seen from the time I started working Border Patrol. But she was the only one I killed because of a set-up and a death wish."

Iris had gotten very quiet. He glanced up at her. "What?"

"All the flame drugs are hard on fetuses."

Back in his human life, he remembered the fuss women would pay to either expectant mothers or infants. It seemed to hurt Iris deeply that the woman had lost her child in utero. But then, he'd come to know Iris as a sensitive, caring woman.

When his phone rang, he wasn't surprised. He reached across the table and drew it close. It was the station.

He kept it on speaker. "Connor."

"You in one piece?" Lily's voice again.

"I am, but let me spare you. Easton needs me out at Tonopah Bridge, right?

"How the hell did you know that?"

"I'm becoming clairvoyant." He heard her laugh, but before she could say anything else, he asked. "What are the details?"

"A bunch of vampires are out there, partying with some flame. Easton wants you to check it out, subdue them if you can."

"Is the canal water still flowing down there?"

"So you knew that as well, huh? But, yeah. They blew enough of a hole to set the water flowing beneath the bridge. That's all I know. Did Vaughn reach you?"

"Yep. But listen, Lily, would you tell Easton something for me?"

"Sure."

"Tell him to go fuck himself."

Lily didn't say anything for a moment. "You sure that's what you want me to do?"

"Oh, yeah. Tell him to go fuck himself and that after I take this call, I'm turning in my badge."

"It's about time. I'm hanging up now because I intend to deliver this message personally."

~~ * ~~

Iris dressed slowly and with great care. She put her hair in a ponytail, donned a pair of black jeans, a reinforced belt, and a hot pink t-shirt because she was pissed. Both their bosses were happy to sell them down the river.

Fine. Whatever.

And Connor had been right to resign. She was thinking about doing the same.

She checked her Sig then clipped on her holster. Her nerves were jumping by the time she met Connor in the dining area.

Damn, but he looked good. The size of his muscles stood out along with his tattoos. He was in full warrior mode with his fighting energy pulsing through the room.

He hadn't changed his clothes since he was basically in uniform already with a black tank, leathers, and heavy boots. He'd pulled the top half of his hair back in a leather strap, the rest of his dark wavy hair touching his shoulders.

He clipped on his Glock and his short-sword, the length more like a long dagger. But the width gave it a deadly weight. The handle and cross-guard were both silver, the sheath a tooled black leather. It was a beautiful, frightening weapon. She hoped he wouldn't have to use it tonight.

As she moved toward him, he nodded. "You don't have to go. In fact, I wish you would stay here and let me deal with this monster."

"I'd like nothing better but my witch instincts are shouting at me. I need to go, so I'm going."

He nodded again. "And we're going to do everything we can to survive."

She drew a deep breath as she watched him buckle on his wrist guards, also in black leather and also heavily reinforced with steel. "I need to show you something before we leave."

"Lead the way."

She headed toward the open French doors and waved for him to join her.

Once standing in the middle of the grass, she looked up and swept her hand in a path over the night sky. "What do you see?"

Connor came up behind her and settled a hand on her left hip. She loved the contact, despite the battle they were headed into.

"I'm not sure what I'm looking at. Do you mean the spell?"

"Yes."

"Huh. I'm seeing a silver pattern that wasn't there before. What is it?"

"It's you."

"What do you mean?"

She turned to face him. "I mean that it showed up after we made love." She wondered how she could explain this. "Earlier, I called to you, remember?"

"Yes. I'd just seen the footage of Rotten Row."

"Right." She flipped her wrist skyward once more. "This is what I wanted to show you. Can you think back to what it felt like right after you fed from me?"

He smiled. "I was pumped."

"Well, this is the result."

He looked up again and she watched his gaze search through the spell, following the intricate silver lines from the tree to the house then back. "It is me, isn't it?"

"Very much so."

"What the hell does it mean? I'm not a wizard. I don't have those powers."

"But you have something similar when you're with me, almost like a mirror. That's what I'm trying to tell you. This is about us, what we seem to have created together. And no, I don't have an explanation or even a thought about what it could mean, the ramifications or potential.

"What I do know is that when we were escaping Gary's club, we had excellent rapport."

"I would agree. Are you suggesting all of this could translate into something in the field?"

"I think so. I just don't know what it would look like or how we'd do it."

He held out his arm to her, and with his free hand gestured to his foot. "Hop on. It's time we head over to Tonopah Bridge and find out."

She didn't hesitate, but stepped up onto his booted foot. Balancing both of hers on just his right foot this time, she then slung an arm around his neck.

The moment he pulled her against his waist, he took off nearly as fast as when the bridge had exploded. What amazed her was how comfortable she'd grown with levitation and flight in what was a very brief twenty-four hour period.

He flew higher as well so she had a unique, bird's eye view of Five Bridges. In the protected areas, street lamps illuminated every row of houses, all the corner stores, gas stations and shopping centers. But soon the land gave way to pits of darkness. The edges of their world, in the middle of north Phoenix, was lit with giant moving spotlights all around the perimeter of the five territories. These lights helped the citizens of Five Bridges to know exactly where the U.S. Border was.

The National Guard had troops stationed on permanent assignment to keep the *alter* species contained. It didn't mean they couldn't get out, but it was getting harder to escape. Elaborate tunnels had become the main exit points.

As a TPS officer, she was fortunate to have a passport and could come and go on stated business. Ironically, she rarely desired to leave Five Bridges. Her home, her life, was here.

The trip across Elegance took less than a minute since Connor was a quick flyer. He chose to make another pass over Sentinel Bridge. A construction crew must have worked through the day using human labor because she could smell the asphalt being laid right now. "That was fast."

"Lots of drug money combined with motivation. Works miracles every time."

Passing into Crescent, however, jump-started her adrenaline. Her vision sharpened, and her muscles had started their own flex-and-release right alongside Connor's.

"How far out?"

"About fifteen seconds."

They passed over a grocery store parking lot filled with vehicles. She had the odd thought that while some of these vampires might be headed in to buy bread, milk and vegetables, she was hoping her man didn't have to use his sword tonight.

She shifted her gaze away from the life she didn't have and engaged the life before her. The canal appeared, crisscrossed by several smaller bridges. He flew above the water then began to slow.

What Iris saw first was an inky witch spell that blotted out the stars and covered the canal as well as the bridge. She could see what looked like a growing stream running in a broad ditch that ran beneath Tonopah Bridge alongside the canal. She realized the ditch had once been part of a run-off landscaping provision for the heavy monsoon months. Her world had simply blasted out a few hundred extra yards which meant the water was rising fast.

Beside the growing stream, several vampires had gathered around a fire they'd built. They were laughing, a couple of them shouting. No doubt they'd been drinking heavily and she suspected were already high on one of the many flame drugs.

"Is that a spell?" Connor asked quietly, drawing her gaze back to the bridge.

"Yes, it is. But I don't know all that it's hiding."

Some of the black smoke on the bridge dissipated suddenly, enough to reveal a lean figure, dressed all in black. He stood balanced on the bridge railing, legs spread wide, his leather duster flapping in the light breeze.

He held a sword in his hand similar to the one Connor owned.

Connor flew slowly in the direction of the vampire and as he did, Iris focused on the spell. It was evil in nature, a conjuring of one of the dark witches. Her heart hammered in her chest.

"This is oppressive," Connor murmured.

"It is. But keep going."

"I am. We need to face our enemy."

Iris swallowed hard as the distance to the bridge shrank. Evil surrounded them now.

But when Connor was only thirty feet from the bridge, the spell shrouding the vampire's face, dissipated.

Iris stiffened in his arms. "Oh, my god, I know him."

"You do?"

"It's Evan. Evan Pierce. Connor, I think I understand the connection and it all makes sense now. The woman you shot and killed had to be Evan's wife, Heather."

CHAPTER SIX

Connor halted midair, fifteen feet away from the man he'd seen at Gary's club. His eyes were green and glinting with a terrible light, something that went beyond a sole need for revenge. Evan was enjoying himself, the control he had over them both right now, and that he'd surprised them.

"So, you're the moral Border Patrol officer above taking the usual bribes."

Connor saw no reason to deny who he was. "I am."

Evan frowned slightly, his gaze fixed on Connor.

Every warrior instinct Connor possessed rose to high alert. Now that he faced his enemy, the man intent on killing them both, adrenaline flooded his veins. His gaze made a sweep of the man, his stance, the relaxed state of his hands, the way he held himself.

Evan had confidence, more than he should if he was alone and facing a seasoned BP officer.

Which meant, Evan had someone with him.

The dark cloud hanging over the entire area, including the vampires partying below, confirmed Connor's belief the man had been corrupted by a witch. Or maybe it was the other way around.

Evan shifted his gaze to Iris. "So, we meet again, yet under very different circumstances."

"You don't need to do this, Evan. We were friends, once, remember?"

"Well, that was before you helped kill my wife."

"You know I did no such thing."

"Oh, but you did. You ended the investigation." Evan continued in this vein, apparently wanting Iris to know how badly she'd failed him.

With Evan's attention shifted away from him, Connor was able to focus on Iris. She was in an unusual state and seemed relaxed yet every sense she possessed had reached out to her environment, including the spell. She might be talking with Evan about past events, but she was analyzing everything around her.

It seemed odd he knew this, but Iris had been trying to tell him something similar in the garden and he began to get what she meant. He shared a connection to Iris now, an awareness of her intentions and her desires.

Evan addressed Connor once more. "You were more directly involved, having shot my wife in the chest point blank."

Connor knew it would make no difference at all, but he said it anyway. "Killing Heather destroyed something inside me. I want you to know that. She was anguished when she died, emaciated because her handlers had her strung out on blood flame. But her last words hurt the worst." He didn't say what they were.

Evan's footing slipped slightly, his eyes widening. He regained his balance, making use of levitation, to once more stand on the metal railing of the bridge. "Her last words? None of my extensive research turned up any such thing. You're lying."

"I was the one there, Evan. I had to look into her beautiful, despairing green eyes. I heard each word she spoke." He slapped a hand against his chest. "They live in here. They always will."

"What did she say?"

Connor debated telling him. If Evan was motivated to hear his wife's final words, that could work in their favor. "I want you to forgive Iris for her failure to keep Heather's case alive. From what I understand, she worked tirelessly to find your wife. Others above her shut the case down. They're to blame. Iris was just doing her job. So, let her off the hook, then I'll tell you."

A hot wind blew suddenly against his back and Iris's arm tightened around his neck. He felt it as well that Evan's witch was making her presence known.

Connor continued. "Your *friend* doesn't seem to like the idea. Is this really up to her?"

Evan's gaze shifted away, his lips turning down.

Iris whispered, "She's communicating with him."

"How?"

"Telepathically, I think."

"Is that something you can do?"

"No. That is. I've never tried. Never even thought about it."

Evan's shoulders had lost their straight edge and his nostrils flared. His lips turned down as he addressed Connor. "Fuck Heather's last words."

"Just as I thought. Pussy-whipped by a witch."

The hot wind slammed so hard into his back he lurched forward, lost his levitating balance and Iris slipped off his boot.

He caught her quickly around the waist, holding her against him, then levitated straight up going as fast as he could. He had one intention, to get Iris the hell out of there.

But he didn't get far. The spell stopped his ability to think in its tracks. He barely knew where he was. He began to descend slowly and the more he did, the clearer his mind became. He attempted a lateral escape, but the same thing happened. The witch had them penned in.

There was no escape now and there would be no reasoning with Evan, no more bargaining, nothing. This would be a battle to the death.

Iris loosened her hold on him and leaned back. She glanced at Evan then back at him. "You do what you've gotta do." She then pushed hard enough to disrupt his hold on her waist so that she fell away from him, letting go of him completely.

"Iris," he shouted, as she fell backward. He started after her, but the hot wind was a wall now and wouldn't let him get to her.

Just as Iris would have hit the side of the ditch, she righted herself in the air. Holy shit, she'd levitated. A few of the more powerful witches and other species could do the same, but it was rare. Or maybe it was her connection to Connor, the mirror-effect she'd talked about earlier.

"I'm okay," she called to him, dropping to balance herself in the rocky dirt. "I suggest you take this asshole out. Evan used to be a good man, but he's no longer here."

Connor didn't have to think twice. He drew his gun and fired repeatedly. But Evan waved a hand and the bullets appeared to fly around him. More witch power, but how was he doing it? How was a vampire accessing the witch's abilities?

Connor holstered his Glock then moved in swiftly, flying to the bridge and dropping down on the pavement. He drew his short-sword from its sheath. Evan's lips curled back in a grimace. He rotated his shoulders and lost his duster. He was lean, but bulked up.

He grabbed his own sword, lowered his shoulders and knees, a smile forming on his lips. "I've been waiting for this for a long time."

"Then you never thought Iris and I would die from the blast?"

"There was a chance, but my woman said Iris was special and didn't have the usual prejudices against vampires that most witches do. She was right. And it's made the game a lot more fun."

"What's your witch's name?" Maybe if he knew who he was battling, he could figure out how to beat Evan.

"None of your business. Besides, she's a very private individual. She wouldn't want her name known."

"She's using you, Evan."

The hot wind rushed into him again, striking once more from behind. He flew forward, rolling hard. He landed on his back at Evan's feet. His sword had been knocked from his hand and Evan's blade was now at his throat.

"Not smart to anger a woman." In a swift move, Evan swept the sword up, reversing direction to bring the rounded hilt end down on Evan's skull.

Connor blinked twice, then nothing.

~~ * ~~

Iris hid under the bridge in a temporary spell she'd built. It wouldn't last long. The other witch's power circled almost endlessly in the entire area. Across the stream, the vampires drank, shouted, and danced around the fire.

Iris had a bad feeling about where all this was building. But she'd already called Lily at the Crescent station, explained what was happening and requested Vaughn as back-up. Lily said she was on it.

Tears touched her eyes. She couldn't hear Connor's voice anymore. Instead, Evan and the witch talked quietly.

She knew Connor wasn't dead, because she could sense his life-force. She could only suppose he was unconscious.

The wind suddenly blew in her direction beneath the bridge. The next moment, her own spell peeled away and Evan was right there, levitating in front of her.

He grabbed her with his powerful arms then pulled her with him as he flew backward. He moved so fast, she couldn't even fight him. Instead, she worked hard just to hold her balance. She even tried to engage her newly realized levitation ability, but couldn't. If he released her now, she'd fly off and probably be crushed by the blow.

Instead, she saw the vampires and the fire below her and the next moment, Evan flung her in the dirt. "Enjoy her, boys. She's yours for the night." He glanced at Iris, his green eyes manic. "Now you'll get to experience how my wife was raped over and over."

Turning, she saw that Connor lay face down in the dirt, wincing as he came back to consciousness. He was too far away to reach, at least twelve feet.

Two of the vampires leaped on Iris. They smelled like whisky and there was a sharp blood flame tang in the air as well. For a moment, she was pinned down, but the vampires were out of control and began hitting each other, vying for first rights.

She gathered her witch energy, sending it down her arm and into her hand. The victor jumped on her, and began pulling at her jeans.

She slowly started to rise to a sitting position, holding her hand steady, her gaze fixed on his temple. All she had to do was touch him in this vulnerable spot or at the base of his neck and he'd die.

But Evan leaped in her direction and grabbed her arm. He clucked his tongue. "None of that or I'll have to hurt you myself." He then took her arm in both hands and lifted his knee.

He looked down at her. "You get a choice. Do I break your arm or do you behave?"

"I'll be good." If he'd broken her arm, the pain would immobilize her completely. From her peripheral vision, she saw that Connor was on his feet, but she didn't look in his direction. She needed to keep Evan focused on her. "Please, don't hurt me, Evan. I swear I won't use my killing power."

Evan smiled and the partying vampire resumed his efforts to get Iris's pants off.

~~ * ~~

Connor no longer had either of his weapons, but he saw his chance and took it. He flew straight at Evan, pulled the man's sword from his sheath, and rammed the blade into his stomach. Evan fell onto his back, grabbing his abdomen, and crying out in pain. Gut wounds were the worst.

Connor then turned and flew behind the vampire still fumbling with Iris's pants and used the same blade to cut his throat.

The other vampires began to move away from him in different directions. He chased one into the muddy stream, who landed on his back. Connor planted his booted foot on the bastard's chest and held him under the water. He drew his sword back, ready to use the blade again.

But the vampire rose up and threw Connor into the air. The sword flipped out of Connor's hand and disappeared into the water.

Connor levitated, then dove at the vampire, shoving him once more into the muddy stream. He punched him in the throat hard, then pushed him under the surface once more, this time sitting on his chest. The vampire struggled, as much against the pain of having his windpipe shattered as trying not to drown. Connor kept him pinned until there was no more movement. When he stood up, the vampire began slowly drifting with the rushing stream.

"Connor!" Iris's hoarse voice called to him.

Connor flew back to the fire and found Evan, white-faced, sitting in the dirt, but with a powerful arm wrapped around Iris's throat. He was trembling from the pain he was in, yet he still had control of Iris. The black cloud boiled above them.

"You come near me, and I'll snap her neck."

One of the remaining vampires suddenly attacked Connor, throwing him into the dirt on his back. Before Connor could move, the vampire landed on his chest and began punching him, in rapid blows. Hopped up on flame as the vampire was, each strike carried unbelievable weight.

Connor tried to move but couldn't.

Iris, he called to her from his mind. He didn't expect anything to return, but he made the effort anyway. The blows began to feel soft, which meant he was sliding into unconsciousness.

He had to do something or Iris would die. And Evan would probably torture her first.

The vampire sitting on him was breathing hard and had stopped punching. It took work to beat the shit out of someone and druggies by nature of their addiction usually weren't in the best shape.

The silver streaks in Iris's spell came to mind. He and Iris had connected in a way he suspected was very similar to Evan and his witch. He focused on Iris, on her witchness, on how much he could sense what she was feeling.

Her voice entered his mind. *Try my killing power, Connor.*

How? Was he really communicating with her telepathically?

He heard Evan's voice. "Your boyfriend is dying. But, look. His vampire opponent is using his smarts. He's picked up a rock."

Connor knew the time had come or this would be his last breath.

He thought back to how he'd felt when he'd fed from Iris and he let that sensation flow through him once more.

Power began to race down his right arm, vibrating with what had to be a witch's killing energy.

The drunk vampire lifted the rock and at the same time, Connor rose up, surrounded his neck with his hand and pressed two fingers into the base of the vampire's skull. The killing energy flowed.

The vampire froze, eyes wide. The rock fell to the ground beside Connor and the vampire slumped over, dead.

Connor jumped to his feet, ready to take on the last of the drugged-out crew. But the vampire was so wasted, he sat and stared at the fire, oblivious.

That left Evan. But when he turned in Iris's direction, she lay on the ground. Alone. Had Evan killed her?

He looked around, waiting for Evan or his witch to strike, but both were gone, including the inky cloud that had surrounded the bridge and the ditch. He thought he understood. The witch had been forced to use her energy to save Evan and couldn't engage in battling either of them. She'd no doubt hauled Evan away to heal him.

In the distance, he saw another vampire heading toward him, but it was Vaughn. Connor could finally breathe.

He turned all his attention to Iris. He knelt beside her and checked to see if she was still breathing. She was, thank God.

He gently felt along each arm and leg to see if anything was broken, but she was okay.

He picked her up, cradling her with her head against his chest then turned to face his brother in arms. "Did Lily send you?"

Vaughn nodded. "But only after your witch called her."

He was taller than Connor, at least six-six. He had steel-gray eyes, straight brows and wore his short black hair shaved at the sides to reveal tattoos on his scalp. Like Connor, he wore a black tank and leathers.

Vaughn scowled as he dipped his chin in Iris's direction. "So what's going on here?"

Connor saw Vaughn's mistrust. He told him everything, start to finish, including the fact he'd slept with Iris, and if he survived whatever this was, he planned to continue being with her.

Vaughn looked appalled then confused. "I sort of get it. I mean, it sounds like she's saved your ass a couple of times."

"She has, but it's more than that." He glanced down at her. She was still unconscious. "I'm in love with her. And we share some kind of bond I can't explain. The weird thing is, I think Evan and his witch are connected in the same way."

Vaughn shook his head and waved both his hands in front of Connor. "I'm sorry. This is too fucking much. Her kind has taken out how many of our friends with that killing power they have?"

"I know." It was a lot to process and he didn't expect Vaughn to come around based on Connor's sudden professed love for a witch.

Vaughn pivoted to take in the scene. "So, where is Evan? You said you gutted him? The vampire should be dead."

"I know, but I think his woman took him away."

"Did you see her?"

"No. She'd be-spelled the entire area." Connor told him about the wind that kept hitting him and knocking him out of stride.

Vaughn scrubbed his fingers through his thick, short black hair. "I've called in a couple of our men. They'll be here in a few and we'll take care of this mess." He offered a half-smile. "You need some healing time, my friend, because you should see your face."

Connor could only guess since it was swollen all to hell. "No doubt. But could you do one thing for me?"

"Sure."

"My weapons are on the bridge."

"I'll be right back." Vaughn launched into the air and returned half-a-minute later with the Glock and the short sword in hand.

Because Connor had Iris in his arms, Vaughn slid the Glock back into its holster, then carefully returned the sword to its sheath.

Connor thanked him and exchanged one last dip of his chin, then rose in the air and headed south toward Elegance.

~~ * ~~

When Iris woke up, she was in Connor's arms and flying. Evan hadn't killed her after all. She didn't think he was physically able to at the end. He'd been losing blood and strength.

Her attention, however, hadn't been focused on him, but rather on the series of blows Connor had taken to his face by the vampire sitting on his chest.

She couldn't believe the moment when Connor had touched her mind. She'd told him the only thing she could think of, that he should try and engage her killing power.

And he had!

A miracle was going on between them and it was beyond her comprehension. She released a heavy sigh.

And suddenly, his thoughts were there, inside her mind again. *How are you feeling?*

It seemed like such a simple thing to respond with telepathy. *Better thanks. Are you okay?*

I will be once the swelling goes down and I get rid of this headache.

Evan didn't cut you, then? When he had you on the bridge?

No. He had other plans. He wanted me to watch those vampires rape you.

He's insane.

I'd have to agree.

But you hurt him. Do you think it's possible he died?

Connor didn't respond right away. *I don't know. That witch has a lot of power.*

She sighed once more.

We're almost home.

She couldn't help but smile that he said 'we'. She loved it. However, she was worn out from the stress of battling the vampires and not knowing when and where either Evan or the witch would strike. She was intensely relieved, however, that they'd made it out alive.

She rubbed his chest and his shoulder. Aloud, she said, "I'm glad you're okay."

He began to slow and the next thing she knew he was descending into her garden. He sat against the tree as he'd done before. Only this time, she could feel him embracing the healing of her sissoo, her shrubs and her plants almost as fully as she was.

Glancing up at him, she saw that he leaned his head against the trunk and his eyes were closed. She watched as the swelling began to dissipate quickly.

Her own wounds were very minor, just the bruising from being handled roughly.

When she felt restored, she looked up at the spell and saw that the silver streaks belonging to Connor were even more prominent and that made her smile. They were sharing powers now.

She thought back to seeing Evan again for the first time in nine or so years. Given the relatively small size of Five Bridges, she should have seen him long before now. Which meant Evan had been living a secret life in the *alter* world probably with the help of his dark witch girlfriend.

Connor had been right; Evan wasn't really interested in justice. He'd become a killer. Maybe his grief had begun the process, but the *alter* transformation had taken his unbalanced mind the rest of the way.

"Thinking about Evan?" Connor's voice rumbled against her ear.

"Yes."

"Me, too. Earlier, he could have killed me on the bridge. He had his sword at my throat." He related what had happened while she'd been attempting to hide out.

"So, why didn't he?"

"He wanted me to see you hurt by those vampires. That was where his pleasure lay."

"You're right. He was bleeding badly from his abdomen, but he sat up and forced me to watch you being hit." She thought for a moment. "And I agree with you. I don't think he's dead either."

"Probably not. His witch is no doubt healing him as we speak. Although it seems like an oxymoron, a dark witch healing anything."

Iris smiled. "I don't think the worst of the witches are about defining anything as good or bad, only what serves their self-interest. Death can be of use to them, so can life. It's a twisted moral system."

"You're right." He leaned down and kissed her forehead. "I'm almost healed up myself, but I'm sitting in wet leathers and I'd like to get out of them."

"Of course." She rose to her feet, though she already missed cuddling with him.

She had it bad.

He took her hand. "How about we get cleaned up together?"

There was a look in his eye as he led her through the open French doors of the bedroom, into the hall, and across the threshold of the way-too-small bathroom.

She smiled as she stripped off her hot-pink t-shirt and savored the way his gaze settled heavily on the mounds of her breasts. She put her hands beneath them and pushed them up and together, creating a deep line of cleavage.

He groaned. He'd been unbuttoning his leathers, but apparently couldn't refuse her invitation. He slid his hands behind her back, dipped his head then spent a serious minute kissing her breasts and tonguing the cleavage between.

She cooed her appreciation, but finally released her girls to attack his pants herself. The leather wasn't cooperative so he suggested she get rid of the rest of her clothes while he pulled off his boots, peeled down his leathers, and lost his tank.

She'd already set the shower to running so that by the time she was undressed and the water was warm, he was in a beautiful naked state, his clothes in a pile. She set her hair loose from her ponytail, then hopped in, sliding beneath the spray and moaning.

"I love the sounds you make." He eased himself into the small tub as well.

"The warm water feels wonderful."

There was barely room for him alone, which meant she had to let him squeeze by her in order to reach the water. He had to do a serious knee bend to get his hair wet. He'd been in the muddy stream so she handed him her favorite sage shampoo.

As he worked the dirt from his hair, her gaze fell to his cock. Because he was busy getting clean, she allowed herself a good long look. He was in a half-aroused state which she thought one of the best looks on a man. This led to other ideas. Grabbing the bar of soap, she lathered up then began to fondle.

He'd been washing his hair with brisk hands but the moment she began a slow glide from the tip of his stalk to the base, he froze and met her gaze.

"Feel good?"

He merely smiled as he continued to lather and rinse, but he kept his gaze on what she was doing.

She played with him, teasing the rim with her soapy thumb then all the way to the tender tip. She kept doing this until he was making a chuffing grunt at the back of his throat. He was fully erect and her body started getting yet another brilliant set of ideas that would involve planting her feet on the edge of the tub and climbing on board.

But he finished rinsing off and gestured for her to take his place. "Your turn, Iris. Get under the water because I want you clean."

The meaning of his words was not lost to her and she clenched deep inside. As she moved to stand beneath the spray once more, he picked up the bar of soap and worked up a lather.

He spent a good amount of time rubbing her sex, and gliding his fingers inside.

She clung to his heavily muscled arms. The warm water on her back, the sight of his tattoos and his damp hair all worked on her. She hadn't had a man in her life for such a long time.

His fingers went faster, working her like a piston. "Can you come like this, Iris? I'd like to watch you come and feel your body pulling on me."

She nodded, her lips parting. But she couldn't quite speak. She let one word slip from her mind to his. *Faster.*

His brows rose, letting her know he'd heard her. And his fingers confirmed it.

He went vampire fast so that after three breaths, she was digging her nails into his arms and crying out.

"That's it, baby. I like to watch you come. That's it, keep it going." He sustained the rhythm, dragging out the orgasm until it passed.

She was left feeling wonderfully lethargic. He withdrew his fingers and slid his arm around her waist to support her. He pulled her close, angling them both into the water. He splashed the spray in her direction and used his hands to get the soap off her, then shut the water off.

What she loved was he never lost contact as he helped her from the shower, making sure she didn't slip. Even when he reached for the towel, he kept a hand on her hip. Afterward, he took his time drying her from head to toe.

Once again, she saw the kind of husband he must have been to his wife, even though it was such a long time ago. "I feel almost human when I'm with you, Connor. Does that sound weird?"

"I get it. This feels almost normal."

She nodded. "Like being with my husband." She wondered if it was the wrong thing to say.

He held her gaze, and stopped moving the towel. "It makes me wish for impossible things."

She took the towel from him. "I know what you mean."

She covered his hair with the towel, tamping it dry, then worked her way down his shoulders and both arms. She drew a ragged breath. She didn't want to think about the future. Five Bridges was a wreck and then there was this dark spot on Connor's soul.

Her own heart was still so full of pain she wondered just how successful a relationship with him could be when so much grief held her captive. "I don't trust love in this world."

"I know. It feels like we're asking too much."

As she wiped his chest, he leaned down and caught her lips with his. She gave a small cry and wrapped her arms around his neck. They'd survived another encounter with a madman and were both alive.

After a moment, he drew back and finished toweling off. When he was done, he took her once more by the hand. He led her straight across the hall, flipped the covers of her bed back so that mostly they ended up on the floor.

"I want you on your back, but first put your ass right here." He patted the edge of the bed.

She moaned as she all but rolled onto the bed. He dropped to his knees and slid his arms under her thighs. Iris couldn't believe this was happening. And what she especially loved was how comfortable he was with her.

For two warring species, they shared a phenomenal amount of trust.

He kissed and tongued her navel, which set her hips rocking. She loved his touch, everything he did to her.

He kissed his way down her abdomen until he reached her bare sex. More kisses, then his tongue.

She drew in a soft stream of air as he pushed between her folds and began to lick.

Her whole body rolled and she cried out. The sensation was so perfect, so full of pleasure.

She swore she'd forgotten the real delights of sex. The few men she'd dated had gone through the motions and left her cold. But maybe that had been her fault because of the way her heart hurt and still felt shut down.

Yet with Connor, she was lit up from within and felt his energy riding her entire body. *Connor.* His name slipped from her mind.

He stopped to look up at her. *It feels so strange to hear you inside my head.*

She lifted up on her elbows and caressed his face. *Same here. I love what you're doing, by the way. It feels amazing. Maybe I can return the favor.*

A wicked glint entered his eye as he began to kiss and lick her once more. *Maybe. In a minute. I'm busy.*

She chuckled and eased her shoulders back down on the bed. *She closed her eyes and savored. He knew his way around a woman's body. When he pierced her well and began to tongue-fuck her in earnest, she couldn't help that her whole body undulated.* Part of her wanted his cock, but the other part loved that he was using his tongue.

Her body grew tense once more. "Faster. Please."

When he began to move at a speed a mere human couldn't manage, she found herself grateful for the vampire he was. Her pelvis tilted and pleasure began to flow, an intense grip in her well, then rushing in a powerful wave up through her abdomen. She cried out and kept crying out. He never let up, sustaining the drive of his tongue until the orgasm passed and her hips melted into the bed.

"Amazing."

He leaned back on his heels, looking up at her, his hands now on her thighs. He looked so gorgeous, his eyes glittering. She sat up and caught his face with her hands, then kissed him, an expression of gratitude for taking care of her. "Thank you. That was beautiful."

He nodded, searching her face. "I loved doing that for you."

When he kept stroking her thighs, she kissed him again. He held her gaze, searching her eyes, then pushed her long, damp hair away from her face. "You're beautiful, Iris."

She sighed. "And your eyes are incredibly blue. I hardly have words to describe them."

He rose up and grabbed her underneath her arms then moved her farther up the bed. She bounced when he dropped her. She loved it.

~~ * ~~

Connor had wanted Iris in this position, on her back and ready for him, since the moment he'd pulled out of her on the lawn. He was sure once he entered her again, he'd want to stay there for a week, hell, a year.

He couldn't explain his drive toward her. On some level he'd thought if he spread her legs and spent his seed deep within her sex, he'd be free to move on.

But he didn't want to. He wanted to stick and that had surprised him. Nothing about Five Bridges invited permanence. Life was more about staying alive than planning a future, especially as a Border Patrol officer.

The past twenty-four hours with Iris had meant more to him than the last thirty years of his life. The trouble was, he wanted more. And more.

He kissed her breasts, taking his time until her body was undulating all over again. He lifted up and caressed her waist and hips, then took his cock in hand.

Yes. Once more her voice floated through his head.

He met her gaze, teasing her opening with the tip of his cock. *You want this?*

She smiled. "More than I've wanted anything in a long time. I want you inside me, driving deep, your energy floating over me again. And one more thing … " She rubbed her fingers up and down her throat. "If you're hungry, I'd love to feed you."

He groaned and pushed at the same time, piercing her sex with his cock. As he moved inside her, he stroked her throat with his fingers. "I'd love to."

A smile infused her entire face. "Good. Because feeding you rocks my world."

Becoming a vampire, especially against his will, had disgusted him in the beginning, especially his drive to take from the vein. When he'd gotten the hang of things, and developed a craving for sustenance, he'd grown more comfortable with the process.

But feeding from Iris had taken him to a whole new level and made him glad, for one of the few times in his life, for the *alter*.

He drove deep inside her and she gasped then met his hips with a serious push of her own. He thrust steadily, caressing her face and kissing her, letting her know with each touch how much she meant to him. If another part of him rose up to remind him he didn't deserve her, he shut it down fast.

This time was for him, however long it lasted. And he intended to take it.

Kissing a line down her throat, he smelled her blood. It was like a fresh breeze on a hot day, so different from any other woman he'd fed from. He licked her throat and her whole body responded in a seductive roll, a confirmation she wanted to feed him.

His fangs descended and he angled just so, then sunk the sharp tips deep. She cried out, gasping. He formed a seal around the wounds and began to drink.

He knew what to expect but the flavor of her blood and the energy that accompanied it surprised him all over again. His hips moved faster. She surrounded him with her arms.

I love this, Connor. More than you can know.

Me, too. And I love that I can talk to you while I'm doing this. Your blood, Iris, it does something amazing to me. I can't explain it. I'm feeling power and sex, a drive for things I'd never thought possible.

I know what you mean. Feeding you is like walking beneath the sun again. And your cock. You feel perfect inside me, made for me.

He was breathing hard as he worked her sex and sucked on her vein. As before, his muscles began to grow pumped and the core of his being felt as though he could do anything.

In this moment, he realized he was ready for life to take him in an entirely new direction. In a way, it already had. He was making love to a witch, something he never thought he'd do.

He drew back from her vein, swiping the wounds with his tongue to seal them. He looked down at her, his hips rocking into her. "Iris, I know this will sound crazy, but will you marry me?"

Her eyes widened. "Connor, is that what you want?"

"It is."

Sudden tears filled her eyes. "Then I will."

He smiled as he rolled his hips. "Not even a single doubt?"

She caressed his face, his shoulder, his arm. "No, not even one."

"Then we're engaged." Once more his guilt rose up, threatening to undo him, but he repressed all the accompanying thoughts and terrible images of his past crimes. He didn't deserve Iris, but for these few minutes or hours, he would pretend he could have her as his wife.

She leaned up to kiss him. He followed her back down, returning the kiss and sliding his tongue inside her mouth.

She held him tight, embracing him with both arms. He moved faster and felt her sex pulling on him. *Are you ready?*

I am.

Faster?

Yes, please.

He could feel her smiling as he kissed her, then lifted up so he could watch her face. He moved faster now, slamming into her. Her fingers kneaded the muscles of his arms, and her hips moved with him, then against him until finally she arched her neck and screamed.

The sight of her ecstasy tightened his balls and his release came like an exquisite fire pulsing through him. With each pump of his hips, he gave to Iris what he felt belonged only to her now.

The pleasure opened his throat and he roared, his hips pumping until the last of his seed left his body. She'd grown lax as well, her arms no longer around him but arranged haphazardly on the bed as though she couldn't hold them up.

Her eyes were at half-mast.

"Was it good for you?" He wanted to hear her say it.

"Absolute heaven." She lifted a lazy arm and pushed his hair back.

He kissed her again. "So, you'll marry me?" He was being foolish but he didn't care.

"Uh-huh. I will. This is the first time in ten years I've felt more like myself and actually hopeful for the future."

She'd said it right. "I feel the same way. But it's crazy, isn't it?"

Connor had a sudden overwhelming need to tell her about the night of the massacre, to confess his worst sin. But he didn't want to ruin the moment, not when he was still connected to her physically and she looked so satisfied.

~~ * ~~

Later, Iris lay in bed and pulled the quilt over her. Connor was showering and she'd follow after. She ran her hands over the nubby texture, the color scheme of the various squares mostly in pinks and greens. She'd bought it many years ago at a flea market before her abduction. The quilt was also one of the things she'd brought with her to Five Bridges from her human life.

When Connor returned, he was frowning. He gestured to the second bedroom. "The door was open and I had a look inside. Iris, did you have a baby?"

The question took her by surprise and without warning tears flooded her eyes. She nodded, then told him about being pregnant during her *alter*.

He came to sit beside her on the bed and took her hand. "I'm so sorry. Christ, you lost your husband and a baby, then your sister. How did you bear it?"

"With great difficulty. But my friend and mentor, Eliza, helped me a lot."

He sighed, holding her gaze. "This is good between, us right?"

"It's wonderful."

He rose to get dressed. "The shower's all yours. But when you're done, we should talk." He looked so serious.

"I won't take long."

As she gathered her things, then moved into the bathroom, she wondered how many times Connor had come close to death in his line of work. Was it possible he'd chosen to work the border, one of the most difficult jobs in their world, because he had a death wish?

Earlier, she'd wanted to address what she perceived as the darkness in his soul, but the moment had been too wonderful. Maybe he was thinking the same thing and the time had come.

If they were to be married, she needed to know what was going on.

When she was done cleaning up, she returned to her bedroom, but Connor wasn't there. She heard what sounded like the TV. Maybe he was checking the news.

She dressed in a fresh pair of jeans and another short-sleeved t-shirt, this one in red. Brushing out her hair, she bound it once more in a ponytail.

Making her way to the living room, she saw Connor standing near the kitchen, but he looked shocked-out again. "Iris, I'm sorry—"

"What do you mean?"

As she moved into the dining area, she saw that the TV wasn't on after all. Then she felt a terrible presence; a dark witch was in her home.

She walked slowly, her heart beating hard in her chest. Her protective spell had been disrupted after all. Reaching the point of the hall where she could see into her living room, Evan and one of the most infamous witches of Elegance came into view. Seraphina.

"Don't be alarmed, my dear," Seraphina said. "We're only here to make sure you knew about Connor."

She was dressed in a floor length, black velvet gown, had long, curly auburn hair and a pure white complexion. Her eyes were black as well. They might have been a different color when she first became a witch, but the kind of craft she practiced, sometimes darkened the eyes. She was tall with a straight nose, perhaps a beauty in her day. Now her features looked hard and vicious.

The witch continued, "I mean that Evan and I can tell you've developed a fondness for the vampire, as I have for my most beloved Evan. But you should know the truth about Connor before you get too involved." She turned to the man whose arm she held. "Wouldn't you agree, darling?"

Evan smiled as he met her gaze. "Absolutely." He shifted his attention to Iris. "We felt it imperative you knew everything." He gestured to Connor. "Though I think he should tell you. My guess is he's been trying to, but couldn't find exactly the right time to share what he did to your sister."

Connor scowled at Evan. "What do you mean, Iris's sister?"

"Oh, yes. She was there. Isn't this somehow poetic?" He gestured to the table. "She's the one with you in the top photograph. That's Violet. She and Iris went through the *alter* together."

Iris's heart beat hard in her chest, hammering away. She knew instinctively that what Connor would say next had to do with the very thing she was most concerned about, the blackness in his soul. "Connor? Is he talking about the massacre in the Graveyard, where Violet died?"

"My memory of that night is sketchy at best. But Evan has showed me the photos." He waved a hand to the table. "Please tell me that's not Violet."

She moved with leaden feet in the direction of a pile of eight-by-ten photographs. She recognized her sister, the life gone from her eyes. Connor was near her, naked, the red flames on his throat indicating he was high, and his fangs dripping. He'd been at the massacre, the one where Violet had been tortured, raped and killed.

CHAPTER SEVEN

Connor stood in a state of shock. He hadn't moved since Evan and Seraphina had pushed through Iris's spell and strolled casually into her living room. They'd been smiling. Evan had even lifted both hands as if in surrender. "We come in peace."

But Seraphina had carried the folder tucked beneath her arm and set it on the dining table. And after flipping it open for him, she spread the photos out.

He'd recognized the location at once, the cement walls and floor of a partially blasted out building. A dozen women had died that night and he'd been part of it. Though to this day, he didn't know all that he'd done.

Now Iris knew about his worst crime. Only it was far worse than he could have ever imagined, because her sister, Violet, had been among the slain witches. Guilt over the massacre swamped him all over again.

He'd been foolish as hell to think his life could be different. But at least Iris now saw him for the monster he was. He felt the waves of her shock and her hatred for his kind boiling in the space between them.

Seraphina addressed Iris. "Don't take it too hard. Connor is after all a vampire first, then a man. He couldn't resist taking out his true nature on something as lovely as your sister. You must forgive him, you know." Then she laughed, a loud trill that set his nerves on fire.

Evan caressed the hand still holding his arm. "I think our work here is done, my love."

"I believe it is. And we should definitely give these two some time to talk things out."

With that, a black cloud filled the room and like something from a cheap movie, the pair disappeared, the cloud with them.

Iris's gaze was still fixed on the sight of her sister in the top photo. Violet's eyes were blank and empty, her skin a pure white, her body covered in blood. Connor forced himself to move forward, then gathered up the photos and shoved them back into the folder, closing it.

"Iris—" he began, but nothing followed. The horror of his existence in Five Bridges fell on him like a heavy weight, pressing him down, closing his throat.

"You did this to Violet? To my own sister?"

"I don't know." He shook his head. "I was there. I know I was there, but my memories of the event aren't complete. I've hated myself for this, for my part in hurting these women."

"Why did you do it?"

"I didn't choose to do this. I was abducted by one of the Rotten Row death squads and shot up with a high dose of blood flame. I don't remember anything after that, just random images of chaos and violence." He could recall the screams of the women, the hard laughter of the men. At some point he'd passed out, and when he'd woken up at home, he had no idea how he'd gotten there. He'd been beaten almost to the point of death.

She gestured to the now closed folder. "There was blood on your fangs and my sister was dead. I think it's clear what happened."

"I know." He sat down in the nearest chair, his mind fixed on that night, trying to remember. But it was blurred like hearing and seeing the whole thing underwater between empty stretches of nothing.

He felt himself falling into a familiar pit, only this time, he wouldn't be able to crawl back out. He'd fallen in love with Iris, but it looked like he'd raped and killed her sister. There was nothing for him here, not now, not ever. He'd been a fool to begin to hope. This was Five Bridges where everyone's soul came to die.

"Get out," Iris said quietly. He felt her killing power rising, but he wasn't going to let her suffer later remorse for taking his life. Because of what they'd shared, she'd have guilt if she killed him.

He rose, numb to his feet, and slowly levitated into the garden. If Evan and his witch were waiting for him, so much the better. They could have him. He was dead now, a hollowed out vampire waiting for the mortal blow.

He levitated swiftly toward the sissoo. Behind him, he heard Iris scream her rage and as he began to rise in the air, a terrible wind of power beat at him. Her killing drive had risen to its highest point. If she'd been close to him, she would have taken his life.

He rose swiftly, then hovered well above her garden. Grief slammed into him over and over at what he'd done, at his life, at all that he'd lost.

"Just as I'd hoped. Iris kicked you out for good." Connor glanced around. He could hear Evan, but he couldn't see him. He realized then that Seraphina's dark cloud hung heavy in the air once more.

He moved in a slow circle midair. "What do you want now? You've already killed me."

The cloud parted enough for Evan to show himself. He was ten feet away, his green eyes glittering. "Not quite, my friend, but we're getting close. I just want you to know that I think you're involvement with Iris, that you'd become lovers, is incredibly poetic and perfect. When I hired the death squad to arrange the massacre and to include Violet, I had them take you along as well for the fun of it. By then, I knew you were the one who shot my wife. I also knew you thought of yourself as a moral Border Patrol cop, and I decided you needed a reality check. I think the massacre had just the right effect.

"But it never once crossed my mind you might actually fall for Iris. In a way, I think it's beautiful."

So, Evan had arranged the massacre to take Violet's life and to mess with Connor's mind. "You were punishing Iris even back then?"

"And you as well, of course."

"You are fucking out of your mind."

Evan lifted both hands and several rough looking vampires suddenly filled the space between him and Evan.

"Don't worry, they're not here for you." Evan signaled to them and they began their descent. "They'll give Iris a few minutes to cool down, then we'll take her as well."

Glancing into the garden, Connor saw that Seraphina was below, working her magic to keep Iris's spell disabled.

In the weight of his guilt and remorse, he'd left Iris alone and unprotected.

Instinctively, he reached for his sword, but it wasn't there. He hadn't taken it with him or his Glock.

Evan laughed softly.

Connor saw movement from the corner of his eye and suddenly Evan was next to him as well as two more vampires who grabbed his arms. He tried to fight them, but the dark cloud suddenly descended, confusing his mind. A split-second later, he felt a sharp prick in his neck.

A fiery chemical entered his body.

Once more, nothing.

~~ * ~~

Iris sat at the dining table. She'd opened the folder and wept at the sight of her sister.

She felt ill. She'd made love with the man who'd killed Violet. He'd probably raped her as well.

Rage rose once more, swirling through her. She wanted revenge on Connor and on Evan as well, on anyone involved in her sister's murder.

Iris, you must listen.

The female voice was strident, not gentle like before. Iris grew very still. *Violet?*

Yes, but you don't have much time. Look at the pictures again. You've missed something critical.

Iris opened the folder once more, to the photo of Connor and Violet in the same picture. Connor's fangs dripped with blood. To the right of him was a severe bite on a thigh, the flesh ripped out, leaving a gaping, bleeding hole.

But it wasn't Violet's thigh!

She stared at it for a long moment. The skin of the victim was very white, but not as though the body had been drained of blood. This was the pale skin of drug-induced emaciation, the kind involving the use of blood flame.

She kept staring at the wound, knowing she needed to figure something out. Then she understood. She wasn't looking at a woman's thigh, but a man's, a vampire's.

"Oh, my God." Connor had been trying to protect Violet, maybe the others as well. In this case, he'd used his fangs as a weapon to tear at the rapist's leg.

She flipped through several of the other photos and found one of Connor lying on his back though only his side, arm and shoulder were visible. In fact, she wouldn't have recognized the man as being Connor if she hadn't known his tattoos as well as she did. The upper right shoulder bore a large spiked vine and she knew every point and angle of the intricate design, as well as where it rested on his body.

But his skin showed severe bruising, a lot of it.

Save Connor. Violet's voice once more moved through her mind. *Don't you see? He tried to help us and they almost killed him for it. Save him, Iris.*

She sat back in her chair, stunned. She thought back to seeing the horrified look on Connor's face and feeling the depth of his despair. He believed he'd participated in the massacre as well and hated himself for it.

This was the darkness that lived in his soul, what she'd been sensing from the moment she'd stood beside him on Sentinel Bridge. He actually believed he'd done these terrible things, that he'd hurt and killed some of these women.

He'd tried to tell her. In fact, she was sure he meant to, then Evan and Seraphina showed up.

Now suddenly, everything had changed and the photos had enough information to prove not only had Connor been a victim of a crime, but he'd tried to help the women until he'd been beaten almost to death.

Even high on blood flame, he'd proven his character and his worth.

He was innocent after all, but he was also completely in despair. What had been shown to him just now would confirm his long-held belief of his unworthiness. He couldn't live with himself if he'd thought he'd killed her sister. And that part of him with a death wish would look for a way to end things.

She had to go to him, to show him the truth, to help him see he'd been lied to.

"You need to work on your spellcasting, Iris. Your protective shield was far too easy to penetrate. But then, I am the most powerful witch in Elegance."

Iris rose to her feet and whirled to face the witch. Seraphina had returned to the living room. Only this time, she'd brought four vampires with her. "Get out of my house."

"Sorry. Can't do that. Not in the plans. But I have to say, I'm a little peeved with you, witch. You've been holding out on your kind. We're always looking for new talent for our coven, and you've got a boatload."

"I'd die first before joining your sick-ass circle."

Seraphina shrugged. "Your choice and as for dying, well, that's a promise." She lifted her hand and snapped her fingers.

When the vampires moved forward, Iris pivoted and raced for the front door.

But as she shifted to turn the knob, one of the vampires caught her from behind, pinning both her arms so she couldn't move.

A prick on her neck followed, as well as the rush of a hot chemical into her skin. Seraphina intended to make good on her promise.

Held tight in the vampire's grip, she was carried outside. She felt the cool night air on her face, then she was airborne.

A moment later, blackness engulfed her.

~~ * ~~

Connor woke up on his side, dizzy as hell. He lay on concrete and felt bruised all over. Maybe he'd fought Evan's men or maybe they'd beaten him up for the hell of it. He didn't know.

Opening his eyes, he squinted. The light, made up of torches, hurt his brain. His mouth was dry and his thirst was off the charts. He had no idea how long he'd been here, wherever the hell 'here' was, since he couldn't see. His vision was blurred.

To his surprise, his hands weren't bound, so he slowly pushed himself to a sitting position. He narrowed his eyes as he looked around, trying to get them to focus. He saw a large shape not far away, but it took him a good minute before he realized he was looking at Iris. She was lying immobile next to a cement wall, her back to him.

He rose unsteadily to his feet and crossed to kneel beside her.

He stroked her hair, then sent words into her mind. *Iris, are you okay? Are you conscious?*

No response. He checked her pulse. She was alive.

They must have drugged her as well.

He took in his surroundings once more, blinking several times. At last his vision cleared fully, but that's when he realized where he was. His stomach turned over as the memories rushed at him, of the women and their screams.

It took him a moment to regain his calm.

Looking up, he checked the sky. There were no stars, just the deep smoke of another spell, undoubtedly Seraphina's.

So, Evan and his witch had brought them here, back to the scene of Violet's death and his crime. He supposed it was fitting, but like hell he would let Iris die here tonight as well.

Though he remained beside her, he extended himself to his environs, feeling the space in a way he knew mirrored Iris's witch abilities. What returned was purposeful and deadly. No more games tonight. The intention was death and of course as much emotional and physical pain as could be inflicted.

His own goal became very simple. He had to protect Iris. Despite that she would hate him now, he had to make sure she lived. He owed that to her as well as to her sister who lost her life at his violent vampire hands.

He drew Iris carefully into his arms. She was completely limp, but breathing.

His heart felt crushed all over again. How much he despised what he'd become. Learning he'd killed Iris's sister had finished him off.

He'd experienced something so rare with Iris that he'd allowed himself a moment to breathe, to feel, to believe maybe he could capture what he'd once had with his wife in the human part of Phoenix.

But he'd been wrong. There was nothing good he could bring to his life in Five Bridges, only heartache and disgust.

He felt deeply resolved to do one thing, and one thing only. And he didn't care if he died in the process. In fact, he welcomed it.

He held Iris close to his chest. "I love you," he whispered. "I've been in love with you for at least seven months. I told you I saw you at the Trib and that was true, but I didn't tell you what made me desire you as much as I did, as I do.

"You looked so serious as you spoke with that woman. I still don't know who she was or what issue had brought her to your office. But she wept and you suddenly dropped down beside her chair and hugged her with both arms.

"That's when I fell in love with you, Iris. You had so much compassion for a witch, for any of our kind in Five Bridges. Seeing you comfort that woman gave me hope.

"And whatever Evan thinks, you don't deserve this. I know you tried to find his wife and I know how much it hurt you to give up the search. Of all the women I know, have ever known, you deserve to live."

He felt movement in the dark spell above him. He shifted his gaze and watched a pair of heavy boots emerge, then a long leather coat, and finally the rest of Evan, who held a short-sword in his hand.

Seraphina followed, her red hair floating as she descended. Once they were both standing on the floor, Evan slipped his arm around her shoulders.

Evan was insane. Connor knew there would be no discussion, no trying to reason with him. It was also possible Seraphina had enthralled

him with a spell and he was under her control. Although, Connor
suspected a spell wasn't necessary.

These two were like minds, a full representation of the darkest parts
of his world. And he was sick of the whole damn thing. Except for Iris.
She had a chance at a real life. She was a good woman and deserved to
live.

"Lovely words you just spoke to Iris." Evan swiped his sword
through the air. "Weren't they, my sweet?"

Seraphina turned into him and caught his cheeks with both hands.
Shaping his lips, she kissed him. "Tender and beautiful. But how did you
know they would fall in love?" She lowered her hand to his chest and
kept it there.

"I didn't. It came as the best surprise. I wanted each of them dead
and wouldn't have minded if the bridge had taken them out. But this is
so much better, isn't it? A real gift."

Seraphina turned her gaze toward Connor, her eyes at half-mast.
"Oh, yes, a thousand times better." She closed her eyes, her lids fluttering.
"To feel their impending loss is absolutely exquisite." She kissed Evan
again, only this time, her lips lingered.

Connor had to look away from so much insanity.

And he had to think.

First things first. He slowly shifted a still unconscious Iris off his
lap, lowering her back to the cement. He arranged her on her side, facing
away from Evan and his witch. He rose to his feet and moved to stand
in front of them.

The couple was still lip-locked.

"Evan," he called out.

The vampire drew back from the impassioned kiss, brows lifted.
"Does my prisoner want something?"

"I do. I want you to let Iris go. She's the true innocent here."

"No one is innocent, Connor. She gave up on my wife and shortly
afterward, you killed Heather. And tonight, you're both going to pay for
what you did."

"You've got me and you can do whatever the hell you want to me. I won't even battle you. I'll lay it all down right now. Just let Iris go."

Evan held his gaze, but his face hardened. "And you think this will do what for me? My wife will still be dead. I can't even get one of the dead-talkers to make contact with her and lord knows I've tried. I probably killed eight or nine of them in the process."

Until this moment, Connor had thought he understood the level of Evan's madness. But he hadn't. "You killed dead-talkers, who are mostly passive and kind? What the fuck is wrong with you?"

Evan, his arm still hanging loose about his woman's shoulders, smiled. "Did you hear that, my love? Connor thinks there's something wrong with me."

Seraphina started to laugh and Evan joined her.

Connor turned to glance down at Iris. She lay prone, but something had changed. He was pretty sure she was waking up.

The time had come. He had to figure out some way to get her to safety.

~~ * ~~

Iris faced a cement wall, torchlight hurting her eyes, probably because of the drug she'd been given. Tears rolled down the side of her face. She'd awakened in time to hear Connor confess how he'd fallen in love with her. And it was pretty much the same reason she'd lost her heart to him. She'd seen his grief over the two children who'd died while caught in the violence of the *alter*, and her heart had been leaning toward him since.

Now they were both held captive by two psychopaths who'd gained power through their coupling.

The cement walls suddenly vibrated with information. She let it come, but the reality hurt her deeply. Violet had died here, in this place along with a lot of other witches. And Connor had been beaten to the point of death. Evan and Seraphina had brought them both back to the scene of the crime.

She heard Seraphina say, "Looks like your girlfriend is waking up."

Iris didn't move, however, but remained on her side staring at the cement wall. She needed to think. She had to formulate some kind of plan.

Violet's death had slanted her own mind, maybe in the same way Heather's death had tipped the scales in Evan's psyche.

Her initial impulse to press her fingers against Connor's temple had been nearly impossible to resist, which was why she'd shouted for him to leave.

Even then, she'd almost flown after him, craving revenge for Violet's death. Yet feeding that beast had cost her how many years of solitude?

She recalled Sadie on the bridge, the red half-heart now like a beacon within Iris's mind.

Her throat grew tight and more tears tracked down her cheeks.

She loved Connor.

She loved him.

And he was innocent of this crime.

Violet, she whispered within her mind, *I understand now what really happened.*

She felt fingertips on her cheeks again.

Violet was here, she was with Iris!

More tears followed. She held her mind open, hoping Violet could tell her something. She heard Connor calling to her, but she remained focused on Violet.

She waited, then Violet's voice was in her mind. *Heather is here with me.*

A jolt went through Iris. She'd heard Evan say he'd killed many dead-talkers for failing to reach his wife. But was Heather really here? Or was Iris in some kind of drugged-out state, conjuring things where they didn't really exist?

But she felt a trail of fingers along her arm that felt very different from her sister's. Then she knew. She was feeling Heather's touch.

It was Heather.

Sweet Christ, what the hell was she supposed to do now?

One thing for certain, it was time to get moving. Slowly, she rose to her feet.

~~ * ~~

The moment Iris stood up, Connor shouted at her. "Stay back. Stay where you are. I won't let Evan hurt you."

Iris answered him in a surprisingly strong voice. "And what about Seraphina? How do you propose to keep a witch from attacking me?" She held her hands out in front of her and looked like she was ready to fall.

He went to her, supporting her around the waist. She turned to look at him, gripping his arm. Tears filled her eyes. "Connor."

"I'm so sorry, Iris. I never thought ... I never meant ... "

She put two fingers against his lips, then slipped into telepathy. *You didn't do it. You didn't hurt Violet or any of the others. Violet told me and the photos support it. You were beaten almost to death, right?*

He nodded.

Violet said you tried to save her and that's why you were hurt. You never touched her.

Tears burned his eyes. "Is it true?"

"Is what true?" Evan asked. "What the hell is going on?"

Connor glanced at the killing pair and watched Seraphina take Evan's hand in her own. She had a shocked, frightened look in her eye. "Don't you see? They're communicating the way you and I do."

"You mean telepathically?"

Connor's telepathy with Iris meant something to the dark witch.

He slid back into Iris's mind. *Do you see Seraphina? She's scared.*

I know. But why is telepathy significant?

I don't know.

"We need to get rid of these two right now." Seraphina's voice had a hard edge.

But Iris called out, "Evan. I have good news for you. Heather is here. I've felt her presence."

Evan stared unblinking at Iris. "What do you mean?"

"Your wife. She's here."

"What's going on?" Connor asked quietly.

She turned to him. "Violet's here as well. They both are." She gestured with a hand to the floor. "Violet died here."

"I know." His shoulders fell. "I woke up in my home with no recollection about what had happened. But my clothes. There was so much blood. I was sick for days. Besides having eight broken ribs and more bruises than I could count. And you're sure I had nothing to do with Violet's death?"

She touched his cheek, then leaned up and kissed him. *Absolutely nothing.*

Seraphina's deep voice intruded. "How touching. But we're off point. Evan, use your blade."

But Evan called out. "What do you mean, Heather is here?"

Seraphina gripped his arm. "Don't listen to her. She's a liar. And why would Heather be here, with Iris, but not with all those dead-talkers?"

Iris turned in his direction. "I felt her presence, Evan. And it was Violet who told me she was here. Both ghosts are present."

Evan's eyes darkened and a heavy frown sat on his brow. "You're a witch, not a dead-talker. Seraphina's right. You're lying."

"I'm not. I felt her touch on my arm."

Evan suddenly grabbed his own arm then looked around. He stepped away from Seraphina and sheathed his sword. "She touched me. I felt it. Heather? *Heather?*" His eyes went wild. "Heather!" he screamed. "I'm here. I'm here." He turned in a circle, his duster flaring out as he moved. "*Heather!*"

Seraphina went to him and settled a hand on his shoulder. Connor thought he would slough it off. Instead, he grew quiet, his vision clouding over.

The witch spoke in a soothing tone. "Calm down, dearest. The witch is lying. She doesn't want Connor to die and she'll say anything to you right now."

Evan turned to her. "But I felt a touch on my arm."

She caressed his face. "You imagined it, my love." She held his gaze. Even from fifteen feet away, Connor could feel Seraphina's witch energy focused on Evan.

He nodded and drew a deep breath. "You're right. I did." He leaned close and kissed her. "Besides, she was my past and you're my present and my future."

"I am."

Connor took Iris's hand. *She's spelled him.*

That she has. She looked up at Connor. *We have a chance right now to end this.*

What do you have in mind?

Not sure, but when I figure it out, I'm taking the bitch down.

~~ * ~~

Iris focused all her thoughts on Seraphina. She'd seen the look of panic in the witch's eyes when Seraphina had realized Iris and Connor were communicating telepathically. But why had she looked so distressed?

Telepathy had to be a power indicator, but what ramification was she missing? Right now, she could communicate with Connor, she could sense him in strong ways, and he could use her killing power. Which meant Iris could probably employ Connor's vampire abilities, but which ones? And how would that work?

Mostly, vampires fed on the blood of others, requiring the substance to live. But what they also had was increased strength, significantly more than either warlocks or witches. If she was right and if she combined these two vampire traits, she suspected she'd have what she needed to battle Seraphina.

Connor, I have an idea about how I can render Seraphina harmless, and she won't be expecting this kind of attack. Also, it may not work, but I want to try. Are you game?

He turned to her, holding her gaze fiercely. *What are you thinking?*

I'm going to bite her and put her in a vampire thrall.

What? His brows rose.

She knew he would start to argue, so she put a hand on his shoulder. *I'm going with my instincts. But the moment I sink my teeth, take Evan down because he'll try to disrupt my attack.*

He gripped her arm in response. *Are you sure?*

Of the outcome? No. That I must try, yes.

He held her gaze for a long moment. *Then do it.*

I want you to protest what I'm about to say. After that, follow my lead. Okay? I love you.

Same here.

Iris turned in Seraphina's direction. "I'll bargain my life and my witch power for Connor's, right now. You let him go, and I'll enter your coven and labor as your servant."

Seraphina released Evan. "Do you hear that, my love? She offers herself in exchange for a vampire."

"Do you believe her?"

"I don't know."

Connor grabbed Iris's arm, pulling her toward him. "Don't do this."

Iris forced tears to eyes. "It's already done." To his mind, she sent, *Get ready to fall and make it look good.* As she pulled away from him, she swept her arms up and created a wind similar to Seraphina's.

Connor stumbled backward and made a show of falling on his ass, then his side. He slid a good eight feet as well.

Iris ignored him and instead moved toward Seraphina. Each step caused her to feel more and more lethargic. The dark witch wasn't taking any chances. She'd created her own spell, one meant to control Iris.

But it gave Iris the exact tool she would need: An appearance of weakness.

She didn't fight Seraphina's spell. Instead, she held out her arms and the moment she drew near, she let out a soft moan and fell toward the woman.

Seraphina caught her and that's when Iris opened her mouth wide and took as much of her throat as she could. She bit down hard.

Seraphina's spell evaporated because Iris's hold on her shifted her focus. She tried to push Iris away, but Iris gripped Seraphina's shoulders as well. Then she bit down even harder until she tasted blood.

And it was that moment, when the metallic flavor hit her tongue, that she felt Connor's vampire ability slam through her, adding his physical strength to the bite.

At the same time, Seraphina became as docile as a lamb. She felt Evan pulling on her shoulders, trying to get Iris away from his woman, but she was part vampire now and she held steady.

His hold didn't last long, either, because Connor had already engaged.

~~ * ~~

At the moment that Evan attempted to pry Seraphina from Iris's arms, Connor levitated swiftly, caught Evan around his waist then twisted him away from the two women. The force he used sent Evan tumbling on the cement.

But Evan rose swiftly in response. He drew his half-sword from his sheath and charged, a wild light in his green eyes.

Connor was unarmed. But he had fifteen years of battling experience, having taken on all kinds of drugged out, hopped up vampires, spellcasters and shifters.

Game on.

Connor held his focus steady, waiting for Evan to make his move. Evan took his time, then finally lunged with a controlled swipe of his sword. At the same moment, Connor levitated backward a foot. Evan came after him with a series of quick cross-swipes that forced Connor to move closer and closer to one of the cement walls.

He knew Evan was trying to back him up against the wall so that Connor couldn't escape the blade. But Connor had been around the block a few times. When he was within a foot-and-a-half from the wall, he used his boot and pushed up and off, levitating swiftly at the same time. He rolled over Evan's head and caught Evan's neck in a chokehold then threw him to the concrete floor.

Evan landed hard and his half-sword went flying. Evan rolled toward it, but Connor was faster, caught the sword in his hand, then shifted course to land on Evan's back. He pressed a knee into his spine.

At the same time, he caught Evan beneath the chin, lifting his head, then brought the sword close to his throat. "You're not much without your witch's help, are you?"

"Fuck you." The words came out slurred because Connor had hold of his chin. Evan wasn't going anywhere.

"You've killed an awful lot of people all in Heather's name. I wonder what she'd think about that."

"She's dead."

"That's true. But you know what else? She's here. You may not be connected to your witch, but I'm in tune with mine and I'm telling you, Heather is here right now. And I think she might have something to say to you. Are you ready to listen?"

Evan grew very still.

"Well?"

"I am."

"Good." He switched to telepathy. *Engage both of us, Heather, right now.*

A female voice pressed into his mind. *Evan, I'm here.*

Heather?

Connor was relieved he could hear them both. Aloud, he said, "I'm going to take the sword away, but I'm keeping my knee in your back. And just so you know, I can hear Heather as well."

"I understand."

Connor slowly moved the sword to the side. *Go ahead, Heather. We're both listening.*

Her voice came through loud and clear. *Evan, you've broken my heart. What have you been doing all in my name and our son's name? We've been waiting for you, but why have you killed so many people? The pain you've caused! That's not who you were. Who we were together.*

Evan's telepathic voice sounded strained. *Heather, I hunted for you. I missed you so much. I'd already made the decision to take a vampire serum so I could look for you. Then I learned that Connor killed you. Why did you have to die? Why couldn't you have waited for me?*

I wouldn't have survived much longer and I couldn't feel the baby move anymore.

Evan didn't say anything for a long moment. *Those were your last words, weren't they? The ones you spoke to Officer Connor? The ones he didn't tell me?*

Yes.

Oh, God, what have I done?

You've hurt so many people and now you have to atone. If you want to be with us, you have to atone.

How?

You'll think of something but now I must go. Connor felt Heather shift her focus, though he didn't understand why until she spoke his name. *Connor, a thousand apologies for using you as I did to take my own life. I didn't realize how much I'd hurt you until Violet told me. Will you forgive me?*

Connor hadn't expected Heather to address anything with him. And Violet was right, Heather's death had ruined something inside his heart. Still, in this moment, he couldn't hold it against her. *This is a hellish world. I only wish I could have saved you that night.*

I didn't know I could trust a vampire. I thought you'd send me back to my abductors.

You had no reason to think differently.

Good-bye, Connor. And Evan, remember, you must atone and do it now. Or I will be lost to you forever. Our son, too.

Connor felt there was something significant in these last words about atoning, but he didn't know what. Maybe her insistence that Evan 'do it now' referred to the location.

The next moment, a soft breeze blew through the terrible space. Heather departed, and the fight left Evan completely.

"I've made a mistake," he said quietly. "You can let me up now."

Connor's cop training made him leery. But his instincts, enhanced by his time with Iris, caused him to levitate off Evan. However, he retained control of Evan's sword.

He flew back slowly several paces, holding his hands wide, the blade secure in his grip, knees bent. If Evan attacked again, he was ready.

But Evan looked wrecked as he stared at Connor. He even looked around the space as though wondering how he'd gotten here. Iris still held Seraphina in a vampire thrall, a very strange thing to see, when she was just a witch. The dark cloud of Seraphina's spell had disappeared as well.

Evan called to the vampires waiting outside the building. When they flew in, he quickly took one of their swords.

Connor moved swiftly in Iris's direction, wondering if he'd just made the worst mistake of his vampire life.

But Evan dismissed the vampires, ordering them to return to their homes. He then drew close to Connor. "When I give the word, I want you to take Iris out of here as fast as you can. We had the place wired." There it was, the reason Heather had told Evan to take care of business now. He understood then what Evan meant to do.

Connor nodded to him. "Let me contact Iris first."

Evan dipped his chin.

He reached for Iris telepathically. *Did you hear Evan?*

Yes.

Do you trust him?

I do.

I'm going to grab your shoulders and pull you out of here at exactly the same time, a single smooth flow of motion. Do you understand and do you trust me?

Yes and yes. Absolutely.

Then we're good to go.

Connor nodded to Evan.

"On three," Evan said, sounding unusually calm. "One … two … three … "

At the same moment that Connor wrenched Iris away, he watched Evan's sword slide into Seraphina's stomach.

Connor pulled Iris tight against him, then flew her swiftly through the doorway and into the air, higher and higher, but arcing southeast toward Elegance.

The explosion followed within three seconds of their departure and was bigger and louder than at Sentinel. This time they weren't directly beneath the blast. However, the ensuing shockwave catapulted them even farther into the night sky.

He didn't try to battle the wave, but flew with it until it dissipated. When they were a full mile distant, Connor slowed his flight, turning them in the air to face No Man's Land. The debris cloud obscured the night and car alarms sounded all over Five Bridges.

Iris held onto him loosely. She watched the cloud, and at the same time wiped her mouth with the back of her hand. She had Seraphina's blood on her lips.

"Did you get any of Heather's telepathy?" he asked.

"Yes. All of it."

"Good." He released a sigh, but not in despair. It was a strange thing to talk to the dead, but both Heather and Violet had given him back his life tonight. What he felt was gratitude, deep eternal gratitude.

"Take me home, Connor."

"No place I'd rather be."

And that was the truth.

Once back in the garden, Iris stared into the face of the man she loved. He'd kissed her about a dozen times, his eyes brimming with tears. He'd professed his love over and over and reaffirmed they were engaged and would soon be married.

She saw how changed he was. The darkness that had held him in its hard grip was now gone. It had been blown away as surely as the blast in No Man's Land had ended Evan and Seraphina's tyranny over their lives.

As she caressed his face, she sought about in her mind for the best way to thank him for coming into her life. Finally, she said, "You've taken all my pain away. Did you know that? I'd grieved for so long. Now all is made new."

He shook his head, searching her eyes. "I'm not sure you could have told me anything better than this. When you enthralled me, and I was able to see all that you were, I felt your pain. You'd lost so much. I also had a wish that one day I could ease your suffering. And if that's what I've done, then I'm happier than I can say."

Iris thought it fitting to take him back into the shower and to clean the debris off their bodies from their final encounter with Evan and his witch. He took her to bed afterward and kept her there for a long time that night and several nights after.

He kept telling her how much he loved her and she returned the favor. She wasn't sure, given all that they'd been through in each of their *alter* lives, that the words could be spoken enough. Iris had never thought to find love in the harsh reality of their drug-riddled world.

But here was Connor, a huge surprise in her life, a blessing sent to her by her sister and to some degree by Heather. If she had one struggle, it was finding exactly the right way to tell Connor how much he meant to her.

Then one day, as Connor began moving his things to her home permanently, she figured it out. And she smiled, because he would love it.

"Iris?" Connor called out to his soon-to-be wife. She'd been in the garage for most of the evening with the Harley mechanic repairing her police cruiser. It needed a new muffler and gas tank and had other assorted dents one of his workers was repairing. Other than that, it had survived the Sentinel explosion really well.

He'd tried several times to head out to the garage to see what was going on. But each time he did, he got sidetracked with another household project. Iris had one helluva list for him, which included putting his Ducati poster up in the living room. But he needed her to eyeball the height for him.

He smiled.

He'd moved in.

A whole week had passed since his announcement that sent about every territory in Five Bridges on its heels. First, he'd made very public his resignation from the Crescent Border Patrol. Then shortly afterward held a press conference with that prick, Donaldson, announcing that he would be the first vampire to join the Tribunal Public Safety force. Donaldson didn't know it yet, but Connor was making it his mission to see the man kicked out of the Tribunal, the sooner the better.

Connor had shaken up Five Bridges but good and at the same time had never felt more alive or more determined to make a difference in his world.

He couldn't believe how much his life had changed.

Not even two weeks ago, he'd been alone, really alone and barely aware how skeletal his life had become. He would be a husband again and once more bound to the obligations of household chores. He couldn't help but smile. Give him chores any day of the week. It seemed an incredibly small price to pay for being with the woman he loved.

And speaking of her, shouldn't her cruiser be repaired by now?

"Iris?" he called out again.

When there wasn't an answer, he got concerned.

He glanced out at the garden, but her latest spell held. Her home was safe. Iris now had a serious witch mentor who tutored her in the ways of fifth level witch-dom. Apparently, her basic power grid was exceptional anyway, but their bond had rocketed her potential into outer space. No dark witch could get through her spell now.

There was also talk she'd one day serve on the Tribunal Council. His chest swelled with a combination of pride and love. Iris had always wanted to make a significant contribution to their world and now she would.

He was about to call her name again, when he decided he'd have to tear her away from her bike himself.

The garage was on the kitchen side of the house. He went through the dining area, but as soon as he got near the door he felt compelled to go back and get the list of projects she'd made up for him.

And that's when it hit him.

Damn. The woman had spelled the garage. He drew closer to the door, fighting the need to reverse direction, and there it was, a line of dragon's blood and something else, probably 'Connor specific', all along the threshold.

"Iris, get your ass in here." He was pissed. She'd promised never to spell him, but she couldn't deny this evidence.

The door opened. She looked like a regular grease-monkey, wearing a kerchief on her head, her ponytail pinned into a bun, and blue overalls. She had the obligatory grease stains smeared here and there. "You spelled this door and you promised me you'd never do that."

She looked sheepish yet pleased at the same time. She was even smiling.

Maybe he wasn't being stern enough. The woman should be contrite.

She glanced over her shoulder. "Duke, I'm in trouble, but do you think he'll forgive me?"

"Hell, yeah, he will."

Connor frowned. "Okay, what's going on?" A row of cabinets prevented him from seeing into the garage.

She reached over the threshold and kicked a break in the line of red powder and the spell dissipated. "Come here," she said. "I have something for you. It's a surprise."

"You're still in trouble."

"I know. I broke a covenant between us, but it was meant for good. You can decide my punishment later. For now, come with me."

When she took his hand, he followed, because he couldn't help himself. She might have spelled him to keep him out of the garage, but her love had become a magnet he didn't think he could ever refuse and that had nothing to do with witchery.

Once he passed the cabinets, he saw all three mechanics, also greasy, but grinning like school kids.

That's when he saw the bike. A Ducati 1974 750 GT. "Iris?"

"She's yours, Connor. The least you deserve for the man you are."

He didn't know what to say. He turned to her, and not caring she was covered in grease, he pulled her into his arms. He kissed her first, then held her so tight he wasn't sure she could breathe.

He wanted to let go, but couldn't. "You've given me so much."

"Same here, my love." She pulled back, her hands on his arms. "But is this okay? Or did I overstep?"

"You mean the Ducati?"

"Yes." She nodded. "And the spell."

"The bike is perfect as well as the intent behind it. Thank you." His heart swelled. He held her gaze once more, not understanding where she'd come from. Iris had only known him a couple of weeks, but seemed to understand him to the depths of his soul. "Thank you."

He then turned to the mechanics who were still grinning. "Well? Does she run?"

They all laughed. Duke said, "You bet she does, but you'll have to sit down and try her out."

Connor went over to the bike and that's when he realized he hadn't heard the engine once. Turning to Iris, he said, "You spelled the sound as well?"

She shrugged. "Kind of had to. You would have known at once this wasn't my TPS bike."

He chuckled. "You're right about that."

He sat down on the seat and kick-started her up. He loved the rumble, the feel, the beauty of it. The vibrations were heaven.

A part of his life had been returned to him.

He thought about taking it out, but dawn was coming and the mechanics needed to be on their way. He shut the engine down, then took his time thanking each of the vampires for the work they'd done.

Iris's cruiser sat in the corner, covered and completely undisturbed.

Duke gestured for his crew to head out through the open garage door and he followed. Connor tracked beside them onto the drive. He looked up into the night sky and up and down the street, but damn if Iris hadn't taken every precaution. He could see her spell all the way to the streetlight about sixty yards away. She'd made sure the vampires were protected from any local, mistrusting witches.

The men hopped on their own bikes and within seconds were

making their way slowly down the suburban street. They knew the drill. They were three Crescent vampires in Elegance and needed to keep a low profile. They could have flown the distance, but each had the same philosophy: Why fly when you can ride?

When Iris came up beside him, he slipped his arm around her shoulders. "Did you give them directions?" she asked.

"Yep, through Revel and Shadow Territories since they're the closest. The last thing these men need to do is cross Sentinel Bridge. The Elegance Border Patrol would probably haul them in for questioning."

"And they might never be seen again."

He turned to her. "You overwhelm me, Iris." He slipped his arms around her and held her close.

She caressed his face. "The Ducati was the least I could do for the man who has so completely changed my life. It seemed like such a small thing when compared to having you in my home and sharing my bed. I don't think I knew how alone I was until you showed up."

He kissed her, a slow tender brush against her lips. When he drew back, he slid his arm around her and led her back to the garage, closing the door.

She gestured to the bike. "You don't want to take her out? She's ready and you've got a few minutes yet."

"I need something else right now."

Since he lowered his hand to fondle her bottom she looked up at him and smiled. "I like your thinking."

When she took his hand, then turned toward the door to the house, he followed after.

"I'm still mad about the spell."

But she only laughed, maybe because he didn't sound convincing.

As she led him past the dining table, she turned to look up at him. "I'm really dirty, Connor. Think you could take me to the shower and get me clean?"

He growled softly. "Definitely."

~~ * ~~

Connor's reaction to the Ducati was exactly what Iris had hoped for. He'd had the strong wind-in-the-face expression she'd wanted, then he'd kissed her.

She knew exactly what the bike meant to him, a symbol of what he'd lost and hopefully what he'd now gained because they'd become a couple, even a team to help build something better in Five Bridges.

The shower was small for his big body, but the cramped space made it fun and close and wonderful. She kept her hands on him the whole time and he returned the favor.

Making love with Connor was better than the sweetest dream. He was an attentive lover, always gauging her reaction to the slightest pressure of his tongue, his fingers, and especially his cock. She worked hard to match him, learning the ways he liked to be sexed up, then brought home.

Then of course, there were times she attacked his body, like now in the shower, for the sheer pleasure of exploring every bulked up muscle he possessed.

After a few minutes of soaping each other, he lifted her up against the tile wall and entered her. She moaned heavily, savoring the connection as he began to drive into her. The water hit them both, another erotic layer of feel-good.

She wrapped her arms around his neck and for just a moment she was reminded of flying with him for the first time.

She held his gaze. "I love you." Then she kissed him.

His whole body responded as he pierced her mouth with his tongue and groaned. He drew back just enough, all the while thrusting into her. "I love you, too, Iris. So much."

He kissed her again, then moved his hips vampire fast, until her mouth opened wide and she screamed the ecstasy that poured through her.

He roared his pleasure at the same time, and their energies merged once more.

When the last pulse settled down, Iris kissed Connor over and over. He stayed connected to her for a long time, doing the same thing.

"I never even imagined you," she said.

"What do you mean?"

"All this time, I'd come to accept the harshness of this life in Five Bridges. Now it's as though an oasis appeared in the middle of a barren desert and I get to live in it. I could never have imagined such a bounty here in our desolate world."

~~ * ~~

Connor finally drew out of Iris, but only because he wanted to take her to bed. He felt a powerful need to spend at least an hour worshipping her body and making her scream repeatedly. He would only be happy when he'd worn her out.

He dried her off and led her to her bedroom, drew the covers back then settled her on the sheets. He made love to her as though this was their last day on earth. He promised himself he'd do the same for the rest of their lives, no matter how many days, months or years would belong to them.

When he'd professed his love repeatedly and she was at last asleep in his arms, the French doors suddenly blew open.

Iris remained asleep, but the smell of thyme filled the air and he could sense Violet's presence once more. He owed the woman everything. She'd stayed behind year after year, until she could resolve a decade of suffering for both him and Iris.

"Thank you," he whispered.

He felt soft fingers down his face. *You're welcome*, swept through his mind. Then, *Tell Iris I love her, but I'm going home now. For good.*

She'll understand. It's what she wants for you.

And let her know I'll be with Anna.

Connor's throat grew tight as he felt the wind sigh and Violet's fingers once more touch his face.

He felt her move over to Iris and watched the slight indentation on her cheeks as Violet touched her for the last time.

The wind blew quickly out of the room, but Violet left the French doors open and for that he was grateful. He could smell the myriad of scents from Iris's garden and each one eased his heart a little more.

He was home now.

After three decades of being on his own, he was home.

Thank you for reading **BLOOD FLAME**! Authors rely on readers more than ever to share the word. Here are some things you can do to help!

Stay connected through my newsletter! You'll always have the *latest releases and coolest contests*! **http://www.carisroane.com/contact-2/**

Leave a review! You've probably heard this a lot lately and wondered what the fuss is about. But reviews help your favorite authors to become visible to the digital reader. So, anytime you feel moved by a story, leave a short review at your favorite online retailer. And you don't have to be a blogger to do this, just a reader who loves books!

Enter my latest contest! I run contests all the time so be sure to check out my contest page today! http://www.carisroane.com/contests/

LIST OF BOOKS

To read more about each one, check out my books page:
http://www.carisroane.com/books/

The Blood Rose Series:

BLOOD ROSE SERIES BOX SET, featuring Book #1
EMBRACE THE DARK, Book #2 EMBRACE THE
MAGIC, and Book #3 EMBRACE THE MYSTERY

EMBRACE THE DARK #1

EMBRACE THE MAGIC #2

EMBRACE THE MYSTERY #3

EMBRACE THE PASSION #4

EMBRACE THE NIGHT #5

EMBRACE THE WILD #6

EMBRACE THE WIND #7

EMBRACE THE HUNT #8

LOVE IN THE FORTRESS #8.1 (A companion book to
EMBRACE THE HUNT)

The Blood Rose Tales:

TRAPPED
HUNGER
SEDUCED

BLOOD ROSE TALES BOX SET

Guardians of Ascension

ASCENSION
BURNING SKIES
WINGS OF FIRE
BORN OF ASHES
OBSIDIAN FLAME
GATES OF RAPTURE

Dawn of Ascension

BRINK OF ETERNITY
THE DARKENING

Rapture's Edge – Continuing the Guardians of Ascension

AWAKENING
VEILED

Amulet Series

DARK NIGHT
WICKED NIGHT

Men in Chains Series (Complete)

BORN IN CHAINS
SAVAGE CHAINS
CHAINS OF DARKNESS
UNCHAINED

Now Available: Book 2 of the Flame Series:

AMETHYST FLAME

http://www.carisroane.com/amethyst-flame-2/

Now Available: EMBRACE THE HUNT, Book 8 of the Blood
Rose Series

A powerful vampire warrior. A beautiful fae of great ability. A war
that threatens to destroy their love for the second time...

http://www.carisroane.com/8-embrace-the-hunt/

Coming Soon: EMBRACE THE POWER, the final installment
of the Blood Rose Series!

Also, be sure to check out the Blood Rose Tales – TRAPPED,
HUNGER, and SEDUCED -- shorter works set in the world of
the Blood Rose, for a quick, satisfying read.

BLOOD ROSE TALES BOX SET

http://www.carisroane.com/blood-rose-tales-box-set/

ABOUT THE AUTHOR

Caris Roane is the New York Times bestselling author of thirty-one paranormal romance books. Writing as Valerie King, she has published fifty novels and novellas in Regency Romance. Caris lives in Phoenix, Arizona, loves gardening, enjoys the birds and lizards in her yard, but really doesn't like scorpions!

www.carisroane.com

YOU CAN FIND ME AT:

Website: http://www.carisroane.com/

Blog: http://www.carisroane.com/journal/

Facebook: https://www.facebook.com/pages/Caris-Roane/160868114986060

Twitter: https://twitter.com/carisroane

Newsletter: http://www.carisroane.com/contact-2/

Pinterest: http://www.pinterest.com/carisroane/

Author of:

Guardians of Ascension Series (http://www.carisroane.com/the-guardians-of-ascension-series/) – **Warriors of the Blood crave the breh-hedden**

Dawn of Ascension Series (http://www.carisroane.com/dawn-of-ascension-series/) – **Militia Warriors battle to save Second Earth**

Rapture's Edge Series (http://www.carisroane.com/raptures-edge/) **(Part of Guardians of Ascension)** – **Second earth warriors travel to Third to save three dimensions from a tyrant's heinous ambitions**

Blood Rose Series (http://www.carisroane.com/the-blood-rose-series/) – **Only a blood rose can fulfill a mastyr vampire's deepest needs**

Blood Rose Tales (http://www.carisroane.com/blood-rose-tales-series/) – **Short tales of mastyr vampires who hunger to be satisfied**

Men in Chains Series (http://www.carisroane.com/men-in-chains-series/) – **Vampires struggling to get free of their chains and save the world**

CPSIA information can be obtained
at www.ICGtesting.com
Printed in the USA
FSOW02n1415101116
27232FS